RIVER OF DEATH

Hamilton knows the way to the ruins, deep in the Brazilian jungle — and the secret they hold. The millionaire who calls himself Smith seeks the lost city to avenge a wrong from his hidden past. Their journey down the River of Death is an epic of violence and danger. But the secret that awaits them in the lost city is more dangerous still — as a legacy of theft, treachery and murder stretching back to war-torn Europe comes to a deadly climax beneath the ancient walls . . .

Books by Alistair MacLean
Published by The House of Ulverscroft:

PARTISANS
ATHABASCA
THE LONELY SEA
NIGHT WITHOUT END

ALISTAIR MacLEAN

RIVER OF DEATH

Complete and Unabridged

ULVERSCROFT
Leicester

First published in Great Britain in 1981 by
William Collins Sons & Co. Ltd., London

First Large Print Edition
published 2013
by arrangement with
HarperCollins*Publishers*, London

The moral right of the author has been asserted

British Library CIP Data

MacLean, Alistair, *1922 –1987*.
River of death.
1. Adventure stories.
2. Large type books.
I. Title
823.9'14–dc23

ISBN 978–1–4448–1391–3

Published by
F. A. Thorpe (Publishing)
Anstey, Leicestershire

Set by Words & Graphics Ltd.
Anstey, Leicestershire
Printed and bound in Great Britain by
T. J. International Ltd., Padstow, Cornwall

This book is printed on acid-free paper

Prologue

Darkness was falling over the ancient Grecian monastery and the first of the evening stars were beginning to twinkle in the cloudless Aegean sky. The sea was calm, the air was still and did indeed, as is so often claimed for it, smell of wine and roses. A yellow moon, almost full, had just cleared the horizon and bathed in its soft and benign light the softly rolling landscape and lent a magical quality to the otherwise rather harsh and forbidding outlines of the dark and brooding monastery which, any evidence to the contrary, slumbered on peacefully as it had done for countless centuries gone by.

At that moment, unfortunately, conditions inside the monastery could hardly be said to reflect the dream-like outer world. Magic had taken wings, no-one slumbered, peace was markedly absent, darkness had given way to a score of smoking oil torches and there was little enough around in the way of wine and roses. Eight uniformed members of the Nazi S.S. were carrying oaken chests across the flagged hallway. The brass-bound boxes were small but so heavy that it required four men

1

to carry one of them: a sergeant supervised their operations.

Watching them were four men. Two of those were high-ranking S.S. officers: of those, one, Wolfgang Von Manteuffel, a tall, thin man with cold blue eyes, was a major-general, no more than thirty-five years old: the second, Heinrich Spaatz, a thick-set, swarthy man who had apparently elected to choose a scowl as his permanent expression in life, was a colonel of about the same age. The other two watchers were monks in cowled brown habits, old proud men but now with mingled fear and pride in their eyes, eyes that never left the oaken chests. Von Manteuffel touched the sergeant with the tip of his gold-handled malacca cane which could hardly have been regulation issue to S.S. officers.

'A spot check, I think, Sergeant.'

The sergeant gave orders to the nearest group who, not without difficulty, lowered their chest to the floor. The sergeant knelt, knocked away the retaining pins in the iron hasps and lifted the hinged lid, the screeching of the ancient metal being testimony enough to the fact that many years must have passed since this had last been done. Even in the wavering light of the malodorous oil torches the revealed contents glittered as if they were alive. The chest contained literally thousands of golden coins, so fresh and gleaming they could have been minted that same day. Von Manteuffel contemplatively stirred the coins with the tip of his cane, looked with satisfaction at the resulting iridescence, then turned to Spaatz.

'Genuine, you would say, Heinrich?'

'I am shocked,' Spaatz said. He didn't look it. 'Shocked beyond words. The holy fathers traffic in dross?'

Von Manteuffel shook his head sadly. 'You can't trust anyone these days.'

With what appeared to be as much a physical effort as an exercise of will, one of the monks averted his fascinated gaze from the glittering chest and looked at Von Manteuffel. He was a very thin man, very stooped, very old — he must have been nearer ninety than eighty. His face was carefully expressionless, but there wasn't much he could do about his stricken eyes.

'These treasures are God's,' he said, 'and we have guarded them for generations. Now we have broken our trust.'

'You can't take all the credit for that,' Von Manteuffel said. 'We helped. Don't worry, we'll look after them for you.'

'Yes, indeed,' Spaatz said. 'Be of good

cheer, father. We shall prove worthy of our stewardship.'

They stood in silence until the last of the treasure chests was removed, then Von Manteuffel gestured towards a heavy oaken door.

'Join your comrades. I'm sure you will be released as soon as our planes are heard to leave.'

The two old men, clearly as broken in spirit as they were in body, did as ordered, Von Manteuffel closing the door behind them and sliding home the two heavy bolts. Two troopers entered, carrying a fifty-litre drum of petrol which they laid on its side close to and facing the oaken door. It was clear that they had been well briefed in advance. One trooper unscrewed the cap of the petrol drum while the other laid a trail of gunpowder to the outside doorway. More than half of the petrol gushed out on to the flags, some of it seeping under the oaken door: the trooper seemed content that the rest of the petrol should remain inside the drum. Following the departing troopers, Von Manteuffel and Spaatz walked away and halted at the outside doorway. Von Manteuffel struck a match and dropped it on the gunpowder fuse: for all the expression that his face registered he could have been sitting in a church.

4

The airfield was only two minutes' walk away and by the time the S.S. officers arrived there the troopers had finished loading and securing the chests aboard the two Junkers 88s, engines already running, parked side by side on the tarmac. At a word from Von Manteuffel, the troopers ran forward and scrambled aboard the farther plane: Von Manteuffel and Spaatz, doubtless to emphasise the superiority of the officer class, sauntered leisurely to the nearer one. Three minutes later both planes were airborne. In robbery, looting and plundering, as in all else, Teutonic efficiency shone through.

At the rear of the lead plane, beyond rows of boxes secured to painstakingly prepared racks on the floor, Von Manteuffel and Spaatz sat with glasses in their hands. They appeared calm and unworried and had about them the air of men secure in the knowledge that behind them lay a job well done. Spaatz glanced casually out of a window. He had no trouble at all in locating what he knew he was bound to locate. A thousand, maybe fifteen hundred feet below the gently banking wing, a large building burnt ferociously, illuminating the landscape, shore and sea for almost half a mile around. Spaatz touched Von Manteuffel on the arm and pointed. Von Manteuffel glanced through the window and almost immediately looked indifferently away.

'War is hell,' he said. He sipped his cognac, looted, of course, from France and touched the nearest chest with his cane. 'Nothing but the best for our fat friend. What value would you put on our latest contribution to his coffers?'

'I'm no expert, Wolfgang.' Spaatz considered. 'A hundred million deutschmarks?'

'A conservative estimate, my dear Heinrich, very conservative. And to think he already has a thousand million overseas.'

'I've heard it was more. In any event, we will not dispute the fact that the Field Marshal is a man of gargantuan appetites. You only have to look at him. Do you think *he* will some day look at *this?*' Von Manteuffel smiled and took another sip of his cognac. 'How long will it take to fix things, Wolfgang?'

'How long will the Third Reich last? Weeks?'

'Not if our beloved Fuehrer remains as commander-in-chief.'

Spaatz looked gloomy. 'And I, alas, am about to join him in Berlin where I shall remain to the bitter end.'

'The *very* end, Heinrich?'

Spaatz grimaced. 'A hasty amendment. Almost the bitter end.'

'And I shall be in Wilhelmshaven.'

'Naturally. A code word?'

Von Manteuffel pondered briefly, then said: 'We fight to the death.'

Spaatz sipped his cognac and smiled sadly. 'Cynicism, Wolfgang, never did become you.'

★ ★ ★

At the best of times the docks at Wilhelmshaven would have no difficulty in turning away the tourist trade. And that present moment was not the best of times. It was cold and raining and very dark. The darkness was quite understandable for the port was bracing itself for the by now inevitable attack by the R.A.F.'s Lancasters on the North Sea submarine base or what, by this time, was left of it. There was one small area of illumination, and subdued illumination at that, for it came from low-powered lamps in hooded shades. Faint though this area of light was, it still contrasted sufficiently with the total blackness around to offer marauding bombers a pinpoint identification marker for the bombardiers crouched in the noses of the planes of the surely approaching squadrons. No-one in Wilhelmshaven was feeling terribly happy about those lights, but then no-one was anxious to question the orders of the S.S. general responsible for their being switched on, especially when that general was carrying with him the personal seal of Field Marshal Goering.

General Von Manteuffel stood on the bridge of one of the latest of the German Navy's longest-range U-boats. Beside him stood a very apprehensive U-boat captain who clearly didn't relish the prospect of being caught moored alongside a quay when the R.A.F. appeared, as he was certain they would. He had about him the air of a man who would have loved nothing better than to pace up and down in an agony of frustration, only there isn't much room for pacing on the conning-tower of a submarine. He cleared his throat in the loud and unmistakable fashion of one who is not about to speak lightly.

'General Von Manteuffel, I must insist that we leave now. Immediately. We are in mortal danger.'

'My dear Captain Reinhardt, I don't fancy mortal danger any more than you do.' Von Manteuffel didn't give the impression of caring about any danger, mortal or otherwise. 'But the Reichsmarshal has a very short way of dealing with subordinates who disobey his orders.'

'I'll take a chance on that.' Captain Reinhardt didn't just sound desperate, he was desperate. 'I'm sure Admiral Doenitz — '

'I wasn't thinking about you and Admiral

Doenitz. I was thinking about the Reichsmar-shal and myself.'

'Those Lancasters carry ten-ton bombs,' Captain Reinhardt said unhappily. 'Ten tons! It took only two to finish off the *Tirpitz*. The *Tirpitz*, the most powerful battleship in the world. Can you imagine — '

'I can imagine all too well. I can also imagine the wrath of the Reichsmarshal. The second truck, God knows why, has been delayed. We stay.'

He turned and looked along the quay where groups of men were hurriedly unload-ing boxes from a military truck and staggering with them across the quay and up the gangway to an opened hatchway for'ard of the bridge. Small boxes but inordinately heavy: they were, unmistakably, the oaken chests that had been looted from the Greek monastery. No-one had to exhort those men to greater effort: they, too, knew all about the Lancasters and were as conscious as any of the imminent danger, the threat to their lives.

A bell rang on the bridge. Captain Reinhardt lifted a phone, listened then turned to Von Manteuffel.

'A top priority call from Berlin, General. You can take it from here or privately below.'

'Here will do,' Von Manteuffel said. He

took the phone from Reinhardt. 'Ah! Colonel Spaatz.'

'We fight to the death,' Spaatz said. 'The Russians are at the gates of Berlin.'

'My God! So soon?' Von Manteuffel appeared to be genuinely upset at the news as, indeed, in the circumstances, he had every right to be. 'My blessings on you, Colonel Spaatz. I know you will do your duty by the Fatherland.'

'As will every true German.' Spaatz's tone, as clearly overheard by Captain Reinhardt, was a splendid amalgam of resolution and resignation. 'We fall where we stand. The last plane out leaves in five minutes.'

'My hopes and prayers are with you, my dear Heinrich. Heil Hitler!'

Von Manteuffel handed back the phone, looked out towards the quay, stiffened then turned urgently towards the captain.

'Look there! The second truck has just arrived. Every man you can spare for the job!'

'Every man I can spare for the job is already on the job.' Captain Reinhardt seemed oddly resigned. 'They all want to live just as much as you and I do.'

* * *

High above the North Sea the air thundered and reverberated to the throbbing roar of scores of aero engines. On the flight deck of the point plane of the Lancaster squadrons, the captain turned to his navigator.

'Our E.T.A. over target area?'

'Twenty-two minutes,' the navigator said. 'Heaven help those poor sods in Wilhelmshaven tonight.'

'Never mind about the poor sods in Wilhelmshaven,' the captain said. 'Spare a thought for us poor sods up here. We must be on their screens by now.'

* * *

At that precise instant another aircraft, a Junkers 88, was approaching Wilhelmshaven from the east. There were only two people aboard, which seemed a poor turn-out for what was supposed to be the last plane out of Berlin. Colonel Spaatz, seated beside the pilot, looked uncommonly nervous and unhappy, a state of mind that was not induced by the fact that their Junkers was being almost continuously bracketed by exploding anti-aircraft shells — practically the entire length of their flight lay over what was now Allied-occupied territory. Colonel Spaatz had other things on his mind. He glanced anxiously at his watch and turned impatiently to the pilot.

'Faster, man! Faster!'

'Impossible, Colonel.'

★   ★   ★

Both troopers and seamen were working in a frenzy of activity to transfer the remaining treasure chests from the second military truck to the submarine. Suddenly, the air raid warning sirens began their ululating banshee wailing. As if by command, and in spite of the fact that they had known this was inevitable, the workers stopped and looked up fearfully into the night sky. Then, once more, again as if by command, they resumed their frantic efforts. It would have appeared impossible that they could have improved upon their previous work-rate but this they unquestionably did. It is one thing to be almost certain that the enemy may appear at any time: it is quite another to have the last lingering vestiges of hope vanish and know that the Lancasters are upon you.

Five minutes later the first bomb fell.

Fifteen minutes later the Wilhelmshaven naval base appeared to be on fire. Clearly, this was no run-of-the-mill raid. By this time Von Manteuffel could have ordered the most powerful arc-lamps, searchlights if necessary, to be switched on and it wouldn't have made the slightest difference. The entire dock area was an inferno of dense and evil-smelling smoke shot through with great columns of flame, through which shadowy Dante-esque figures moved as in some nameless nightmare, seemingly as oblivious of their surroundings as they were of the screaming aero engines, the ear-numbing explosion of bombs, the sharp whip-like cracks of heavy anti-aircraft fire, the ceaseless stuttering of machine-guns, although what the machine-guns hoped to achieve was difficult to imagine. Through all this the S.S. men and the seamen, reduced now, despite all their will to the contrary, to almost zombie slow motion by the increasingly heavy burden of the chests, continued their by now fatalistic loading of the submarine.

On the conning-tower of the submarine both Von Manteuffel and Captain Reinhardt were coughing harshly as the dense and evil-smelling smoke from the burning oil tanks enveloped them. Tears streamed down the cheeks of both men.

Captain Reinhardt said: 'God's sake, that last one was a ten-tonner. And straight on top of the U-boat pens. Concrete ten feet thick, twenty, what does it matter? There can't be a man left alive there now, the concussion would have killed them all. In heaven's name, General, let's go. We've had the devil's own luck till now. We can come back when it's all over.'

'Look, my dear Captain, the air raid is at its height now. Try moving out of the harbour now, a slow business as you know, and you have as good a chance of being blown out of the water as you have alongside the quay here.'

'Maybe so, Herr General, maybe so. But at least we'd be *doing* something.' Reinhardt paused, then went on: 'If I may say so without offence, sir, surely you must know that a captain is in command of his own vessel.'

'Even as a soldier I know that, Captain. I also know that you're not in command until you have cast off and are under way. We complete loading.'

'I could be court-martialled for saying this, but you are inhuman, General. The devil rides your back.'

Von Manteuffel nodded. 'He does, he does.'

* * *

At the Wilhelmshaven airfield a dimly seen plane, later identifiable as a Junkers 88, made so violently bumpy a touch-down that its undercarriage could well have collapsed under the impact. The bumpiness was understandable, the drifting smoke being so intense that the pilot could make only a blind guess as to his height above the runway. Under normal conditions he would never have dreamed of attempting so hazardous a landing but the conditions were far from normal. Colonel Spaatz was a man of a highly persuasive cast of mind. Even before the plane had rolled to rest he had the door open, peering anxiously for his waiting transport. When finally he saw it — an open Mercedes staff car — he was aboard it within twenty seconds, urging the driver to make all possible haste.

★　★　★

The smoke surrounding the submarine was, if anything, even denser and more acrid than it had been minutes before although a sudden gusting wind, no doubt the result of the firestorm, gave promise of an early amelioration of the conditions. But choking and half-blinding though the smoke still was it didn't prevent Von Manteuffel from seeing what, despite his coolly relaxed calm, he had so desperately wanted to see.

15

'That's it, then, Captain Reinhardt, that's it. The last chest aboard. And now your men aboard, Captain, and let the devil ride on *your* back.'

Captain Reinhardt was hardly in the frame of mind to require any second bidding. Shouting hoarsely to make himself heard above the still thunderous din, he ordered his men aboard, ropes to be cast off and engines slow ahead. The last of his men were still frantically climbing up the sliding gangway as the submarine inched away from the quayside. It hadn't moved more than a few feet when the sound of a motor car screeching and skidding to a halt made Von Manteuffel turn sharply and look at the quay.

Spaatz had leapt from the Mercedes while it was still moving. He stumbled, recovered himself, and stared at the still very slowly moving submarine, his face contorted in desperate anxiety.

'Wolfgang!' Spaatz's voice wasn't a shout, it was a scream. 'Wolfgang! God's sake, wait!' Then the anxiety on his face yielded abruptly to an expression of utter incredulity: Von Manteuffel had a pistol lined up on him. For some seconds Spaatz remained quite still, shocked into a frozen and uncomprehending immobility, then comprehension came with the crack of Von Manteuffel's pistol and he hurled himself to the ground as a bullet struck only a foot away. Spaatz dragged his Luger from its holster and emptied it after the slowly moving submarine which, apart from giving vent to his feelings, was an otherwise futile gesture as the conning-tower was apparently empty, Von Manteuffel and Captain Reinhardt having obviously and prudently ducked beneath the shelter of the steel walls off which Spaatz's bullets ricocheted harmlessly. And then, abruptly, the submarine was lost in the swirling banks of smoke.

Spaatz pushed himself to his hands and knees and then stood upright and stared in bitter fury in the direction of the vanished submarine.

'May your soul rot in hell, Major-General Von Manteuffel,' Spaatz said softly. 'The Nazi Party's funds. The S.S. funds. Part of Hitler's and Goering's private fortunes. And now the treasures from Greece. My dear and trusted friend.'

He smiled almost reminiscently.

'But it's a small world, Wolfie, my friend, a small world, and I'll find you. Besides, the Third Reich is gone. A man must have something to live for.'

Unhurriedly, he reloaded his Luger, brushed the mud and moisture from his clothes and walked steadily towards the Mercedes staff car.

The pilot was in his seat, poring over a chart, when Spaatz clambered aboard the Junkers 88 and took his seat beside him. The pilot looked at him in mild astonishment.

Spaatz said: 'Your tanks?'

'Full. I — I didn't expect you, Colonel. I was about to leave for Berlin.'

'Madrid.'

'Madrid?' This time the astonishment was more than mild. 'But my orders — '

'Here are your new orders,' Spaatz said. He produced his Luger.

1

The cabin of the thirty-seater aircraft was battered, scruffy, unclean and more than a little noisome, which pretty accurately reflected the general appearance, of the passengers, who would never have made it to the ranks of the international jet-set. Two of them could have been classified as exceptions or at least as being different from the others although neither of them would have made the jet-set division either, lacking, as they did, the pseudo-aristocratic veneer of your true wealthy and idle layabout. One, who called himself Edward Hiller — in this remote area of southern Brazil it was considered poor form to go by your own given name — was around thirty-five, thickset, fair-haired, hard-faced, obviously European or American and dressed in tan bush-drills. He seemed to spend most of his time in moodily examining the scenery, which, in truth, was hardly worth the examining, inasmuch as it duplicated tens of thousands of square miles in that virtually unknown part of the world: all that was to be seen was an Amazonian tributary meandering its way through the endless green of the rain forest of the Planalto de

Mato Grosso. The second exception — again because he seemed not unacquainted with the basic principles of hygiene — claimed to be called Serrano, was dressed in a reasonably off-white suit, was about the same age as Hiller, slender, black-haired, black-moustached, swarthy and could have been Mexican. He wasn't examining the scenery: he was examining Hiller, and closely at that.

'We are about to land at Romono.' The loudspeaker was scratchy, tinny and the words almost indistinguishable.

'Please fasten seat-belts.'

The plane banked, lost altitude rapidly and made its approach directly above and along the line of the river. Several hundred feet below the flight-path a small, open outboard motorboat was making its slow way upstream.

This craft — on closer inspection a very dilapidated craft indeed — had three occupants. The largest of the three, one John Hamilton, was tall, broad-shouldered, powerfully built and about forty years of age. He had keen brown eyes, but that was about the only identifiable feature of his face as he was uncommonly dirty, dishevelled and unshaven, giving the impression that he had recently endured some harrowing ordeal, an impression heightened by the fact that his filthy clothes were torn and his face, neck

20

and shoulders were liberally blood-stained. Comparatively, his two companions were presentable. They were lean, wiry and at least ten years younger than Hamilton. Clearly of Latin stock, their olive-tinged faces were lively, humorous and intelligent and they looked so much alike that they could have been identical twins, which they were. For reasons best known to themselves they liked to be known as Ramon and Navarro. They considered Hamilton — whose given name was, oddly enough, Hamilton — with critical and speculative eyes.

Ramon said: 'You look bad.'

Navarro nodded his agreement. 'Anyone can see he's been through a lot. But do you think he looks bad enough?'

'Perhaps not,' Ramon said judicially. 'A soupçon, perhaps. A little touch here, a little touch there.' He leaned forward and proceeded to widen some of the already existing rents in Hamilton's clothing. Navarro stooped, touched some small animal lying on the floorboards, brought up a bloodied hand and added a few more artistically decorative crimson touches to Hamilton's face, neck and chest then leaned back to examine his handiwork critically. He appeared more than satisfied with the result of his creative workmanship.

'My God!' He shook his head in sorrowful

admiration. 'You really have had it rough, Mr Hamilton.'

★   ★   ★

The faded, peeling sign on the airport building — hardly more than a shack — read: 'Welcome to Romono International Airport' which was, in its own way, a tribute to the blind optimism of the person who had authorised it or the courage of the man who had painted it as no 'international' plane had ever landed or ever would land there, not only because no-one in his right senses would ever voluntarily come from abroad to visit Romono in the first place but primarily because the single grass runway was so short that no aircraft designed later than the forty-year-old DC3 could possibly hope to land there.

The aircraft that had been making the downriver approach landed and managed, not without some difficulty, to stop just short of the ramshackle terminal. The passengers disembarked and made for the waiting airport bus that was to take them into town.

Serrano kept a prudent ten passengers behind Hiller but was less fortunate when they boarded the bus. He found himself four seats ahead of Hiller and therefore was in no position to observe him any more. Hiller was now observing Serrano, very thoughtfully.

★ ★ ★

Hamilton's boat was now closing in on the river bank. Hamilton said: 'However humble, there's no place like home.'

Using the word 'humble' Hamilton was guilty of a grave understatement. Romono was, quite simply, a jungle slum and an outstandingly malodorous example of the genre. On the left bank of the aptly named Rio da Morte, it stood partly on a filled-in, miasmic swamp, partly in a clearing that had been painfully hacked out from a forest and jungle that pressed in menacingly on every side, anxious to reclaim its own. The town looked as if it might contain perhaps three thousand inhabitants: probably there were double that number as three or four persons to a room represented the accommodation norm of Romono. A typically sleazy end-of-the-line — only there was no line — frontier town, it was squalid, decaying and singularly unprepossessing, a maze of narrow, haphazardly criss-crossing alleys — by no stretch of the imagination could they have been called streets — with the buildings ranging from dilapidated wooden shacks through wine-shops, gambling dens and bordellos to a large and largely false-fronted hotel rejoicing, according to a garish blue neon sign, in the name of the OTEL DE ARIS, some misfortune having clearly overtaken the missing capitals H and P.

The waterfront was splendidly in keeping with the town. It was difficult to say where the river bank began for almost all of it was lined with houseboats — there had to be some name for those floating monstrosities — relying for their construction almost entirely on tar paper. Between the houseboats were piles of driftwood, oil cans, bottles, garbage, sewage and great swarms of flies. The stench was overwhelming. Hygiene, had it ever come to Romono, had gratefully abandoned it a long time ago.

The three men reached the bank, disembarked and tied up the boat. Hamilton said: 'When you're ready, take off for Brasilia. I'll join you in the Imperial.'

Navarro said: 'Draw your marble bath, my lord? Lay out your best tuxedo?'

'Something like that. Three suites, the best. After all, we're not paying for it.'

'Who is?'

'Mr Smith. He doesn't know it yet, of course, but he'll pay.'

Ramon said curiously: 'You know this Mr

Smith? Met him, I mean?'

'No.'

'Then might it not be wise to wait for the invitation first?'

'No reason to wait. Invitation's guaranteed. Our friend must be nearly out of his mind by now.'

'You're being downright cruel to that poor Mr Hiller,' Navarro said reproachfully. 'He must have gone out of his mind during the three days we stayed with your Muscia Indian friends.'

'Not him. He's sure he *knows* he knows. When you get to the Imperial keep close to a phone and away from your usual dives.'

Ramon looked hurt. 'There *are* no dives in our fair capital, Mr Hamilton.'

'You'll soon put that right.' Hamilton left them and made his way in the gathering dusk through winding, ill-lit alleyways until he had passed clear through the town and emerged on its western perimeter. Here, on the outskirts of the town and on the very edge of the forest and jungle, stood what had once passed for a log cabin but was now no more than a hut and even at that, one would have thought, a hut scarcely fit for animal far less human habitation: the grass- and weed-covered walls leaned in at crazy angles, the door was badly warped and the single window had hardly an unbroken pane of glass left in it. Hamilton, not without some difficulty, managed to wrench open the creaking door and passed inside.

He located and lit a guttering oil lamp which gave off light and smoke in about equal proportions. From what little could be seen from the fitful yellow illumination, the interior of the hut was a faithful complement of the exterior. The hut was very sparsely furnished with the bare essentials for existence — a dilapidated bed, a couple of bentwood chairs in no better condition than the bed, a warped deal table with two drawers, some shelving and a cooker with some traces of the original black enamel showing under the almost total covering of brown rust. On the face of it, Hamilton didn't care too much for the sybaritic life.

He sat wearily on the bed which, predictably, sagged and creaked in an alarmingly disconcerting fashion. He reached under the bed, came up with a bottle of some undetermined liquid, drank deeply from the neck and set the bottle down somewhat unsteadily on the table.

Hamilton was not unobserved. A figure had appeared just outside the window and was peering inside from a prudent distance, a probably unnecessary precaution. It is more difficult to see from a lighted area to a darkened one than the other way round and the windows were so filthy that it was difficult to see through them anyway. The watcher's face was indistinct, but the identity of the man not hard to guess: Serrano was probably the only man in Romono who wore a suit, far less an off-white one. Serrano was smiling, a smile composed of an odd mixture of amusement, satisfaction and contempt.

Hamilton extracted two leather pouches from the torn remains of his buttoned pockets and poured the contents of one of them into the palm of his hand, staring in rapt admiration at the handful of rough-cut diamonds which he let trickle onto the table. With an unsteady hand he fortified himself with another drink then opened the other pouch and emptied the contents onto the table. They were coins, glittering golden coins; all told there must have been at least fifty of them.

Gold, it is said, has attracted men from the beginning of recorded time. It unquestionably attracted Serrano. Seemingly oblivious of the possibility of discovery, he had moved closer to the window, so close, indeed, that a keen-eyed and observant person inside the hut might well have seen the pale blur of his face. But Hamilton was being neither keen-eyed nor observant: he just stared in apparent fascination at the treasure before him. So did Serrano. The amusement and contempt had disappeared from his expression, the unblinking eyes seemed huge in his face and his tongue licked his lips almost continuously.

Hamilton took a camera from his rucksack, removed a cassette of exposed film, examined it closely for a moment and, in doing so, dislodged two diamonds which fell and rolled under the table, apparently unobserved. He put the cassette on a shelf beside some other cassettes and cheap camera equipment then turned his attention to the coins again. He picked one up and examined it carefully, almost as if seeing it for the first time.

The coin, indisputably gold, did not appear to be of any South American origin — the likeness of the engraved head was unmistakably of classical Greek or Latin origin. He looked at the obverse side: the characters, clear and unblemished, were unmistakably Greek. Hamilton sighed, lowered some more of the rapidly diminishing contents of the bottle, returned the coins to the pouch, paused as if in thought, shook some coins into his hand, put them in a trouser pocket, put the pouch into one of his buttoned shirt pockets, returned the diamonds to their pouch and his other buttoned pocket, had a last drink, turned out the oil lamp and left. He made no attempt to lock the door for the sufficient reason that, even with the door as fully closed as it would go, there was still a two-inch gap between the key bolt and door jamb. Although it was by now almost dark he did not appear to require any light to see where he was going: within a minute he vanished into the shanty-town maze of corrugated iron and tarpaper shacks which formed the salubrious suburbs of Romono.

Serrano waited a prudent five minutes, then entered, a small flashlight in his hand. He lit the oil lamp, placing it on a shelf where it could not be seen directly from the outside then, using his flashlight, located the fallen diamonds under the table and placed them on the tabletop. He crossed to the shelves, took the cassette which Hamilton had placed there, replaced it with another from the pile of cassettes and had just put the cassette on the table beside the diamonds when he became suddenly and uncomfortably conscious of the fact that he was not alone. He whirled around and found himself staring into the muzzle of a gun expertly and unwaveringly held in Hiller's hand.

'Well, well,' Hiller said genially. 'A collector, I see. Your name?'

'Serrano.' Serrano didn't look any too happy. 'Why are you pointing that gun at me?'

'Calling cards you can't get in Romono, so I use this instead. Are you carrying a gun, Serrano?'

'No.'

'If you are and I find it I'm going to kill you.' Hiller was still geniality itself. 'Are you carrying a gun, Serrano?'

Serrano reached slowly for an inside pocket. Hiller said: 'The classic way, of course, my friend. Finger and thumb on the gun barrel then gently on the table.'

Serrano carefully, as directed, produced a small snubnosed automatic and laid it on the table. Hiller advanced and pocketed it, along with the diamonds and the cassette.

'You've been following me all day,' Hiller said consideringly. 'For hours before we boarded that plane. And I saw you the previous day and the day before that. In fact, I've seen you quite a few times in the past weeks. You really should get yourself another suit, Serrano, a shadower in a white suit is no shadower at all.' His tone changed in a fashion that Serrano clearly didn't care much for. 'Why are you following me, Serrano?'

'It's not you I'm after,' Serrano said. 'We're both interested in the same man.'

Hiller lifted his gun a perceptible inch. If he'd lifted it only one millimetre it would have carried sufficient significance for Serrano who was in an increasingly apprehensive state of mind. 'I'm not sure,' Hiller said, 'that I like being followed around.'

'Jesus!' Serrano's apprehension had become very marked indeed. 'You'd kill a man for a thing like that?'

'What are vermin to me?' Hiller said carelessly. 'But you can stop knocking your knees together. I've no intention of killing you — at least, not yet. I wouldn't kill a man just for following me around. But I wouldn't draw the line at shattering a kneecap so that you couldn't totter around after me for a few months to come.'

'I won't talk to anyone,' Serrano said fervently. 'I swear to God I won't.'

'Aha! That's interesting. If you were going to talk who would you talk to, Serrano?'

'Nobody. Nobody. Who would I talk to? That was just a manner of speaking.'

'Was it now? But if you *were* to talk, what would you tell them?'

'What could I tell them? All I know — well, I don't know, but I'm pretty sure — is that Hamilton is into something big. Gold, diamonds, something like that — he's found a cache somewhere. I know that you're on his track, Mr Hiller. That's why I am following you.'

'You know my name. How come?'

'You're a pretty important man around these parts, Mr Hiller.' Serrano was trying to be ingratiating but he wasn't very good at it. A sudden thought appeared to occur to him for he brightened and said: 'Seeing we're both after the same man, Mr Hiller, we could be partners.'

'Partners!'

'I can help you, Mr Hiller.' Serrano was eagerness itself but whether from the prospect of partnership or the understandable desire not to be crippled by Hiller it was difficult to say. 'I *can* help you. I swear I can.'

'A terrified rat will swear to anything.'

'I can prove what I say.' Serrano seemed to have regained a measure of confidence. 'I can take you to within five miles of the Lost City.'

Hiller's initial reaction was one of astonishment and suspicion.

'What do you know about it?' He paused and recovered himself, 'Well, I suppose everybody's heard about the Lost City. Hamilton's always shooting off his mouth about it.'

'Mebbe so. Mebbe so.' Serrano, sensing the change in the atmosphere, was almost relaxed now. 'But how many have followed him four times to within a few miles of it?' If Serrano had been at the gambling table he'd have leaned back in his chair, his trump card played.

Hiller had become very interested indeed, even to the extent of lowering, then pocketing, his own gun.

'You have a rough idea where it is?'

'Rough?' Immediate danger past, Serrano invested himself with an air very close to benign superiority. 'Close is more like it. Very close.'

'Then if you've come all that close why don't you go looking for it yourself?'

'Look for it myself!' Serrano looked almost shocked. 'Mr Hiller, you must be out of your mind. You don't understand what you're talking about. Have you *any* idea what the Indian tribes in the area are like?'

'Pacified, according to the Indian Protection Service.'

'Pacified?' Serrano gave a contemptuous laugh. 'Pacified? There isn't enough money in the country to make those desk-bound pansies leave those lovely air-conditioned offices in Brasilia and go see for themselves. They're terrified, just plain terrified. Even their field-agents — and there are some pretty tough cookies among them — are terrified and won't go near the area. Well, four of them did go there once some years back, but none of them ever returned. And if they're terrified, Mr Hiller, I'm terrified too.'

'That creates quite a problem.' Not surprisingly, Hiller had become quite thoughtful. 'An approach problem. What's so special about those blood-thirsty people? There are many tribes who don't care all that much for people from the outside, what you and I would regard as other civilised people.' Apparently Hiller saw nothing incongruous in categorising himself and Serrano as 'civilised'.

'Special? I'll tell you what's special about them. They're the most savage tribes in the Mato Grosso. Correction. They're the most savage tribes in the whole of South America. Not one of them has moved out of the Stone Age so far. In fact, they must be a damned sight worse than the Stone Age people. If the Stone Age people had been like them they'd have wiped each other out — when those tribes up there have nothing better to do, they just go around massacring each other — to keep their hand in, I suppose — and there would have been no human left on this planet today.

'There are three tribes up there, Mr Hiller. First, there are the Chapates. God knows they're bad enough, but all they do is use their blowpipes, pump a few curare-tipped poison darts into you and leave you lying there. Almost civilised, you might say. The Horenas are a bit different. They use darts that only knock you unconscious; then you're dragged back to their village and tortured to death — this, I understand, can take a day or two — then they cut off your head and shrink it. But when it comes to sheer savagery, the Muscias are the pick of the bunch — I don't think any white man has ever seen them. But one or two of the outside Indians who have met them and survived say that they're cannibals and if they see what they regard as being a particularly appetising meal they dump him alive into boiling water. Something like lobsters, you know. Go looking for a lost city surrounded by all those monsters? Why don't *you* go looking? I can point you in the right direction. Me, I only like cooking pots from the outside.'

'Well, maybe I'll have to do a little more thinking on that one.' Absently, almost, he handed Serrano back his gun. Hiller was no mean psychologist when it came to gauging the extent of a man's cupidity. Hiller said: 'Where do you live?'

'A room in the Hotel de Paris.'

'If you saw me in the bar there?'

'I've never seen you before in my life.'

* * *

35

An unbiased guidebook to the better taverns of South America would have had some difficulty in finding the space to list the bar of the Hotel de Paris, Romono, in its pages. The bar was not a thing of beauty. The indeterminately coloured paint, what little there was of it, was peeling and blistered, the splintered wooden floor was blackened and filthy and the rough-cut softwood bar bore the imprint of the passage of time. A thousand spilt drinks, a thousand stubbed-out cigars. It was not a place for the fastidious.

The clientele, fortunately, were not of an overly fastidious nature. Exclusively male and dressed for the most part in scarecrow's clothing, they were rough, uncouth, ill-favoured and hard-drinking. Especially hard-drinking. As many customers as possible — and there were many — pushed up to the bar and consumed huge quantities of what could only be described as rot-gut whisky. There was a scattering of bentwood chairs and rickety tables, largely unoccupied. The citizens of Romono were mostly vertical drinkers. Among the currently vertical were both Hiller and Serrano, separated from each other by a prudent distance.

In such surroundings, then, the entrance of Hamilton did not provoke the horror-stricken reaction that it would have in the plusher caravanserais of Brasilia or Rio. Even so, his appearance was sufficient to cause a marked drop in the conversational level. With his tangled hair, a week's growth of matted and bloodied beard, and ripped and blood-stained shirt he looked as if he had just returned from the scene of a successfully if messily executed triple murder. His expression — as was indeed customary with him — lacked anything in the way of encouragement towards social chitchat. He ignored the stares and although the crowd before the bar was at least four deep a path opened magically before him. In Romono, such a path always opened for John Hamilton, a man very obviously held, and for a variety of good reasons, in considerable respect by his fellow citizens.

A large, very fat barman, the boss of the four men serving nonstop behind the bar, hurried forward towards Hamilton. His egg-bald pate gleamed in the light: inevitably, he was known as Curly.

'Mr Hamilton!'

'Whisky.'

'God's name, Mr Hamilton. What happened?'

'You deaf?'

'Right away, Mr Hamilton.'

Curly reached under the bar, produced a

37

special bottle and poured a generous measure. That Hamilton should be thus privileged apparently aroused no resentment among the onlookers, not so much because of their innate courtesy, of which they had none, but because Hamilton had demonstrated in the past his reaction to those who interfered in what he regarded as his own private business: he'd only had to do it once, but once had been enough.

Curly's plump, genial face was alive with curiosity as were those of the bystanders. But Hamilton was not a man to share confidences as everyone was well aware. He tossed two Greek coins on to the bar. Hiller, who was standing close by, observed this and his face grew very still indeed. His face was not the only one to assume sudden immobility.

'Bank's shut,' Hamilton said. 'Those do?'

Curly picked up the two shining coins and examined them with an air of unfeigned reverence.

'Will those do? *Will those do!* Yes, Mr Hamilton, I think those will do. Gold! Pure gold! This is going to buy you an awful lot of Scotch, Mr Hamilton, an awful lot. One of those I'm going to keep for myself. Yes, sir. The other I'll take and have valued in the bank tomorrow.'

'Up to you,' Hamilton said indifferently.

Curly examined the coins more closely and said: 'Greek, aren't they?'

'Looks like,' Hamilton said with the same indifference. He drank some of his Scotch and looked at Curly with a speculative eye. 'You wouldn't, of course, be dreaming of asking me if I went all the way to Greece to get those?'

'Certainly not,' Curly said hastily. 'Certainly not. Will I get the doctor, Mr Hamilton?'

'Thanks. But it's not my blood.'

'How many of them? Who did this to you — I mean, who did you do it to?'

'Just two. Horenas. Same again.'

Although most people at the bar were still looking at Hamilton or the coins, the hubbub of conversation was slowly resuming. Hiller, glass in hand, elbowed his purposeful way towards Hamilton who regarded Hiller's approach with his customary lack of enthusiasm.

Hiller said: 'I hope you'll excuse me. I don't want to intrude, Hamilton. I understand that after tangling with head-hunters a man would like some peace and quiet. But what I'd like to say to you is important. Believe me. Could I have a word?'

'About what?' Hamilton's tone was less than encouraging. 'And I don't like discussing business — I assume it is business — with a dozen pairs of ears hanging on to every word I say.'

Hiller looked around. Inevitably, their conversation was attracting attention. Hamilton paused for a moment, as if in thought, then picked up his bottle, jerked his head and led the way to the corner table most remote from the bar. Hamilton, as always, looked aggressive and forbidding and his tone matched his expression.

'Out with it,' he said, 'and no shilly-shallying.'

Hiller took no offence. 'Suits me. That's the way I like it, the only way to do business. I'll lay it on the line. It's my belief you've found this Lost City of yours. I know a man who'd pay you a six-figure fee to take him there. That straight enough for you?'

'If you throw away that rot-gut rubbish you have there I'll give you some decent Scotch.' Hiller did as requested and Hamilton topped up both glasses. Hiller was clearly aware that Hamilton was less interested in dispensing hospitality than in having time to think and from the just perceptibly slurred note in Hamilton's voice it could well have been that he could be taking just slightly longer than normal to think quickly and clearly.

'Well, I'll say this,' Hamilton said, 'you

don't beat about the bush. Who says I've found the Lost City?'

'Nobody. How could they? No-one knows where you go when you leave Romono — except maybe those two young sidekicks of yours.' Hiller smiled thinly. 'They don't look like the type that would talk too much.'

'Sidekicks?'

'Oh, come off it, Hamilton. The twins. Everybody in Romono knows them. But it would be my guess that *you* would be the only person to know the exact location. So, okay, I'm only going on a hunch — and a couple of brand new golden coins that may be a thousand years old, two thousand. Just supposing.'

'Supposing what?'

'Supposing you'd found it, of course.'

'Cruzeiros?'

Hiller kept his face impassive, a rather remarkable feat in view of the wave of elation that had just swept through him. When a man talks money it means that he is prepared to dicker, to make a deal, and Hamilton had the means to bargain. Hamilton had his *quid pro quo* and that could mean only one thing — he knew where the Lost City was. He had his fish hooked, Hiller thought exultantly: now all he had to do was gaff and land him. That might well take time, Hiller knew, but

41

he had every confidence in himself: he rather fancied his prowess as a fisherman.

'U.S. dollars,' Hiller said.

Hamilton thought this over for a few moments then said: 'An attractive proposition. Very attractive. But I don't accept propositions from strangers. You see, Hiller, I don't know you, what you are, what you do, and how come you are empowered to make this proposition.'

'A con man, possibly?'

'Possibly.'

'Oh, come. We've had a drink a dozen times in the past months. Strangers? Hardly. We all know why you've been searching those damned forests for the past four months and other huge stretches of the Amazon and Paraná basins for the past four years. For the fabled Lost City of the Mato Grosso — if that is indeed where it is — for the golden people who lived there — who may still live there — most of all for the fabled man who found it. Huston. Dr Hannibal Huston. The famous explorer who vanished into the forests all those many years ago and was never seen again.'

'You talk in clichés,' Hamilton said.

Hiller smiled. 'What newspaperman doesn't?'

'Newspaperman?'

'Yes.'

'Odd. I'd have put you down for something else.'

Hiller laughed. 'A con? A convict on the lam? Nothing so romantic, I'm afraid.' He leaned forward, suddenly serious. 'Listen. As I said, we all know why you're out here — no offence, Hamilton, but goodness knows you've told everyone often enough — although why I don't know — I'd have thought you'd have kept it secret from everybody.'

'Three good reasons, my friend. In the first place, there has to be some reason to account for my presence here. Secondly, anybody will tell you that I know the Mato Grosso better than any other white man and no one would dream of following me where I go. Finally, the more people who know what I'm after the greater the likelihood that some person, some time and in some place, will drop a hint or a clue that could be invaluable to me.'

'I was under the impression that you didn't require hints or clues any longer.'

'That's as maybe. Just you go ahead and form any impressions you like.'

'Well, all right. So. Ninety-nine per cent of the people laugh at your wild notions, as they call them — though God knows there's not a man in Romono would dare say it to your face. But I belong to the one per cent. I believe you. I further believe that your search is over and that the dream has come true. I'd like to share in a dream, I'd like to help a man, my employer, make his dream come true.'

'I'm deeply moved,' Hamilton said sardonically. 'I'm sorry — well, no, I'm not really — but something gives here that I just can't figure. And besides, Hiller, you are an unknown quantity.'

'Is the McCormick-Mackenzie International?'

'Is it what?'

'Unknown.'

'Of course not. One of the biggest multinational companies in the Americas. Probably the usual bunch of crooks using the usual screen of a battery of similarly crooked international lawyers to bend the laws any which way that suits them.'

Hiller took a deep breath, manfully restraining himself. 'Because I'm in the position of asking a favour of you, Hamilton, I won't take exception to that. In point of fact the record of McCormick-Mackenzie is impeccable. They have never been investigated, far less impeached on any count.'

'Smart lawyers. Like I said.'

'You can be glad that Joshua Smith is not here to hear you say that.'

Hamilton was unimpressed. 'He the owner?'

'Yes. And the Chairman and Managing Director.'

'The multi-millionaire industrialist? If we're talking about the same man?'

'We are.'

'*And* the owner of the largest newspaper and magazine chain in the Americas. Well, well, well.' He broke off and stared at Hiller. 'So that's why you — '

'Exactly.'

'So. He's your boss, a newspaper magnate. And you're one of his newspapermen, and a pretty senior one at that, I would guess — I mean, he wouldn't send out a cub reporter on a story like this. Very well. Your connections, your credentials established. But I still don't see — '

'What don't you see?'

'This man. Joshua Smith. A multi-millionaire. A multi-billionaire. Anyway, as rich as Croesus. What's left on earth for him that he doesn't already have? What more can a man like that want?' Hamilton took a long pull at his whisky. 'In short, what's in it for him?'

'You are a suspicious bastard, aren't you, Hamilton? Money? Of course not. Are you in it for the money? Of course not. A man like you could make money anywhere. No, and again no. Like you — and, if I may say, a little bit like myself — he's a man with a dream, a dream that's become an obsession. I don't know which fascinates him the more, the Huston case or the Lost City, although I don't suppose you can really separate the two. I mean, you can't have the one without the other.' He paused and smiled, almost dreamily. 'And what a story for his publishing empire.'

'And that, I take it, is your part of the dream?'

'What else?'

Hamilton considered, using some more Scotch to help him with his consideration. 'Mustn't rush things, mustn't rush things. A man needs time to think about these things.'

'Of course. How much time?'

'Two hours?'

'Sure. My place. The Negresco.' Hiller looked around him and gave a mock shudder which could almost have been real. 'It's almost as good as it is here.'

Hamilton drained his glass, rose, picked up his bottle, nodded and left. No-one could have accused him of being under the weather but his gait didn't appear to be quite as steady as it might have been. Hiller looked around until he located Serrano, who had been looking straight at him. Hiller glanced

46

after the departing Hamilton, looked back at Serrano and nodded almost imperceptibly. Serrano did the same in return and disappeared after Hamilton.

Romono had not yet got around to, and was unlikely ever to get around to, street-lighting, with the result that the alleyways, in the occasional absence of saloons and bordellos fronting on them, tended to be very poorly lit. Hamilton, all trace of his unsteady gait vanished, strode briskly along, clearly unbothered by the fitful or nonexistent lighting. He rounded a corner, carried on a few yards, stopped suddenly and turned into a narrow and almost totally dark alleyway. He didn't go far into the alley — not more than two feet. He poked his head cautiously out from his narrow niche and peered back along the way he had just come.

He saw no more than he had expected to see. Serrano had just come into view. Serrano, it was clear, wasn't out for any leisurely evening stroll. He was walking so quickly that he was almost running. Hamilton shrank back into the shadows. He no longer had to depend on his hearing. Serrano was wearing steel-tipped shoes which no doubt he found indispensable for the subtler intricacies of unarmed combat. On a still night Serrano could have been heard a hundred yards away.

Hamilton, no more than another shadow in his shadowy place of concealment, listened to the rapidly approaching footsteps. Serrano, almost running now, looked neither to right nor to left but just peered anxiously ahead in quest of his suddenly and mysteriously vanished quarry. He was still peering anxiously ahead when he passed the alleyway entrance. Hamilton, a shadow detaching itself from the deeper shadow behind, stepped out swiftly and in silence brought his locked hands down on the base of Serrano's neck. He caught the already unconscious man before he could strike the ground and dragged him into the dark concealment. From Serrano's breast pocket he removed a well-filled wallet, extracted a gratifying wad of cruzeiro notes, pocketed them, dropped the empty wallet on top of Serrano's prone form and continued on his way, this time without a backward glance. He had no doubt that Serrano had been on his own.

Back in his tumbledown hut, the guttering oil lamp lit, Hamilton sat on his cot and pondered the reason for his being shadowed. That Serrano had acted under Hiller's instructions he did not for a moment doubt. He did not think that Serrano had intended to waylay or attack him for he could not doubt that Hiller was almost desperately anxious to have his services and an injured Hamilton would be the last thing he would want on his hands. Nor could robbery have been a motive — although they may well have seen the bulges of the two pouches in his shirt pockets — and Hamilton had been well aware that Serrano had been watching him through the hut window — comparatively petty theft would not have interested Hiller; what he was after was the pot of gold at the foot of the rainbow and only he, Hamilton, knew where that rainbow ended.

That Hiller and his boss Smith had dreams Hamilton did not for a moment doubt: what he did doubt, and profoundly, was Hiller's version of those dreams.

Hiller had wanted to find out if he had been going to contact his two young assistants or other unknown parties. Perhaps he thought that Hamilton might lead him to a larger and worthwhile cache of gold and diamonds. Perhaps he thought Hamilton had gone to make some mysterious phone call. Perhaps anything. On balance, Hamilton thought, it was just because Hiller was of a highly suspicious nature and just wanted to know what, if anything, Hamilton was up to. There could be no other explanation and it seemed pointless to waste further time and thought on it.

Hamilton poured himself a small drink — the nondescript bottle did in fact contain an excellent Highland malt which his friend Curly had obtained for him — and topped it up with some mineral water: the Romono water supply was an excellent specific for those who wished to be laid low with dysentery, cholera, and a variety of other unpleasant tropical diseases.

Hamilton smiled to himself. When Serrano came to and reported his woes to his master, neither he nor Hiller would be in any doubt as to the identity of the assailant responsible for the sore and stiff neck from which Serrano would assuredly be suffering. If nothing else, Hamilton mused, it would teach them to be rather more circumspect and respectful in their future dealings with him. Hamilton had no doubt whatsoever that he would be meeting Serrano — officially — in the very near future and would thereafter be seeing quite a deal of him.

Hamilton took a sip of his drink, dropped to his knees, ran his hand over the floor under the table, found nothing and smiled in satisfaction. He crossed to the shelving, picked up a solitary cassette, examined it carefully and smiled in even wider satisfaction. He drained his glass, turned out the light and headed back into town.

In his room in the Hotel Negresco — the famous hotel in Nice would have cringed at the thought that such a hovel should bear the same name — Hiller was making — or trying to make — a telephone call, his face bearing the unmistakable expression of long-suffering impatience that characterised any person so foolhardy as to try to phone out of Romono. But at long last his patience was rewarded and his face lit up.

'Aha!' he said. His voice, understandably, had a note almost of triumph in it. 'At last, at last! Mr Smith, if you please.'

2

The drawing-room of Joshua Smith's villa — the Villa Haydn in Brasilia — demonstrated beyond all question the vast gulf that lay between a multibillionaire and the merely rich. The furnishings, mainly Louis XIV and not the shadow of an imitation in sight, the drapes, from Belgium and Malta, the carpets, ancient Persian to the last one, and the pictures, ranging all the way from Dutch Old Masters to the Impressionists, all spoke not only of immense wealth but also a hedonistic determination to use it to its maximum. But for all that vast opulence there was nonetheless displayed an exquisite good taste in that everything matched and blended in something very, very close to perfection. Clearly, no modern interior decorator had been allowed within a mile of the place.

The owner matched up magnificently to all this magnificence. He was a large, well-built and dinner-suited man of late middle age who looked absolutely at home in one of the huge armchairs that he occupied close to a sparkling pine log fire.

Joshua Smith, still dark in both hair and

moustache, the one brushed straight back, the other neatly trimmed, was a smooth and urbane man, but not too smooth, not too urbane, much given to smiling and invariably kind and courteous to his inferiors which, in his case, meant just about everybody in sight. With the passage of time, the carefully and painstakingly acquired geniality and urbanity had become second nature to him (although some of the original ruthlessness had had to remain to account for his untold millions). Only a specialist could have detected the extensive plastic surgery that had transformed Smith's face from what it once had been.

There was another man in his drawing-room, and a young woman. Jack Tracy was a young-middle-aged man, blond, with a pock-marked face and a general air of capable toughness about him. The toughness and capability were undoubtedly there — they had to be for any man to be the general manager of Smith's vast chain of newspapers and magazines.

Maria Schneider, with her slightly dusky skin and brown eyes, could have been South American, Southern Mediterranean or Middle Eastern. Her hair was the colour of a raven. Whatever her nationality she was indisputably beautiful with a rather inscrutable face but invariably watchful penetrating eyes. She didn't look kind or sensitive but was both. She looked intelligent and had to be: when not doubling — as rumour had it — as Smith's mistress she was his private and confidential secretary and it was no rumour that she was remarkably skilled in her official capacity.

The phone rang. Maria answered, told the caller to hold and brought the phone on its extension cord across to Smith's armchair. He took the phone and listened briefly.

'Ah, Hiller!' Smith, unusually for him, leant forward in his armchair. There was anticipation in both his voice and posture. 'You have, I trust, some encouraging news for me. You have? Good, good, good. Proceed.'

Smith listened in silence to what Hiller had to say, the expression on his face gradually changing from pleasure to the near beatific. It was a measure of the man's self-control that, although apparently in a near transport of excitement, he refrained from either exclamations, questions or interruptions and heard Hiller through in silence to the end.

'Excellent!' Smith was positively jubilant. 'Truly excellent. Frederik, you have just made me the happiest man in Brazil.' Although Hiller claimed to be called Edward, his true given name would have appeared to be otherwise. 'Nor, I assure you, will you have cause to regret this day. My car will await you and your friends at the airport at eleven a.m.' He replaced the receiver. 'I said I could wait forever. Forever is today.'

Moments passed while he gazed sightlessly into the flames. Tracy and Maria looked at each other without expression. Smith sighed, gradually bestirred himself, leaned back into his armchair, reached into his pocket, brought out a gold coin, and examined it intently.

'My talisman,' he said. He still didn't appear to be quite with them. 'Thirty long years I've had it and I've looked at it every day in those thirty years. Hiller has seen this very coin. He says the ones this man Hamilton has are identical in every way. Hiller is not a man to make mistakes so this can mean only one thing. Hamilton has found what can only be the foot of the rainbow.'

Tracy said: 'And at the far end of the rainbow lies a pot of gold?'

Smith looked at him without really seeing him. 'Who cares about the gold?'

There was a long and, for Tracy and Maria, rather uncomfortable silence. Smith sighed again and replaced the coin in his pocket.

'Another thing,' Smith went on. 'Hamilton appears to have stumbled across some sort of an El Dorado.'

'It seems less and less likely that Hamilton

55

is the kind of man to stumble across anything,' Maria said. 'He's a hunter, a seeker — but never a stumbler. He has sources of information denied other so-called civilised people, especially among the tribes not yet classified as pacified. He starts off with some sort of clue that points him in the right direction then starts quartering the ground, narrowing the area of search until he finally pinpoints what he's after. The element of chance doesn't enter into that man's calculations.'

'You might be right, my dear,' Smith said. 'In fact you're almost certainly right. Anyway, what matters is that Hiller says that Hamilton seems to have located some diamond hoard.'

Maria said: 'Part of the war loot?'

'Overseas investments, my dear, overseas investments. Never war loot. In this case, however, no. They are uncut — rough-cut, rather — Brazilian diamonds. And Hiller is an expert on diamonds — God knows he's stolen enough in his lifetime. Anyway, it appears that Hamilton has fallen for Hiller's story, hook, line and sinker — in Hiller's rather uninspired phrase. Two birds with one stone — he's found both the European gold and the Brazilian diamonds. Looks as if this is going to be even easier than we thought.'

Tracy looked vaguely troubled. 'He hasn't

the reputation for being an easy man.'

'Among the tribes of the Mato Grosso, agreed,' Smith said. He smiled as if anticipating some future pleasure. 'But he's going to find himself in a different kind of jungle here.'

'Maybe you overlook one thing,' Maria said soberly. 'Maybe you're overlooking the fact that you've got to go back into that jungle with him.'

* * *

Hiller, in his room in the Hotel Negresco, was studying a gold coin which he held in his hand when he was disturbed by an erratic knock on the door. He pulled out a gun, held it behind his back, crossed to the door and opened it.

Hiller put his gun away: the precaution had been unnecessary. Serrano, both hands clutching the back of his neck, swayed dizzily and practically fell into the room.

'Brandy!' Serrano's voice was a strangled croak.

'What the hell's happened to you?'

'Brandy!'

'Brandy coming up,' Hiller said resignedly. He gave a generous double to Serrano who downed it in a single gulp. He had just finished his third brandy and was pouring out his tale of woe when another sharp rat-tat-tat came on the door, this knocking far from erratic. Again Hiller took his precautionary measures and again they proved unnecessary. The Hamilton who stood in the doorway was scarcely recognisable as the Hamilton of two hours previously. Two hours in the Hotel de Paris's grandiloquently named Presidential Suite — no president had ever or would ever stay there, but it had the only bath in the hotel not corroded with rust — had transformed him. He had bathed and was clean-shaven. He wore a fresh set of khaki drills, a fresh khaki shirt without a rent in sight and even a pair of gleaming new shoes.

Hiller glanced at his watch. 'Two hours precisely. You are very punctual.'

'The politeness of princes.' Hamilton entered the room and caught sight of Serrano who was busy pouring himself another large brandy. By this time it was difficult to judge whether he was suffering the more from the effects of the blow or the brandy. Holding the glass in one rather unsteady hand and massaging the back of his neck with the other, he continued the restorative process without seeming to notice Hamilton.

Hamilton said: 'Who's this character?'

'Serrano,' Hiller said. 'An old friend.' It would have been impossible to guess from Hiller's casual off-handedness that he'd met Serrano for the first time only that evening. 'Don't worry. He can be trusted.'

'Delighted to hear it,' Hamilton said. He couldn't remember the month or the year when he last trusted anybody. 'Makes a welcome change in this day and age.' He peered at Serrano with the air of a concerned and kindly healer. 'Looks to me as if he's coming down with something.'

'He's been down,' Hiller said. 'Mugged.' He was observing Hamilton closely but could well have spared himself the trouble.

'Mugged?' Hamilton looked mildly astonished. 'He was walking the streets this time of night?'

'Yes.'

'And alone?'

'Yes,' Hiller said and added in what he probably regarded as a rather pointed fashion: 'You walk alone at night.'

'I know Romono,' Hamilton said. 'Much more importantly, Romono knows me.' He looked pityingly at Serrano. 'I'll bet you weren't even walking in the middle of the road — and I'll bet you're that much lighter by the weight of your wallet.'

Serrano nodded, scowled, said nothing and got back to his self-medication.

'Life's a great teacher,' Hamilton said absently. 'But it beats me how a citizen of Romono could be so damned stupid. Okay, Hiller, when do we leave?'

Hiller had already turned towards a glass-fronted wall cupboard. 'Scotch?' he said. 'No fire-water. Guaranteed.' He showed Hamilton a famous proprietary brand of Scotch with the seal unbroken.

'Thanks.'

Hiller's gesture had not been motivated by an undiluted spirit of hospitality. He had turned his back on Hamilton to conceal what he knew must have been a momentary flash of triumph in his face; moreover, this was definitely a moment for celebration. Back in the bar of the Hotel de Paris he had been sure that he had his fish hooked: now he had it gaffed and landed.

'Cheers,' he said. 'We leave at first light tomorrow.'

'How do we go?'

'Bush plane to Cuiabá.' He paused then added apologetically: 'Rickety old bus of cardboard and wire but it's never come down yet. After that, Smith's private jet. That's something else again. It will be waiting for us at Cuiabá.'

'How do you know?'

Hiller nodded towards the phone. 'Carrier pigeon.'

'Pretty sure of yourself, weren't you?'

'Not really. We like to arrange things in advance. I just go on probabilities.' Hiller shrugged. 'One call to fix things, then another call to cancel. Then from Cuiabá to Smith's private airfield in Brasilia.' He nodded towards Serrano. 'He's coming with us.'

'Why?'

'Why ever not?' Hiller even managed to look puzzled. 'My friend. Smith's employee. Good jungle man.'

'Always wanted to meet one of those.' Hamilton looked consideringly at Serrano. 'One can only hope that he's a little bit more alert in the depths of the Mato Grosso than he is in the alleys of Romono.'

Serrano had nothing to say to this but he was, clearly, thinking: prudently he refrained from voicing his thoughts.

★   ★   ★

Smith, it would seem, was both a considerate man and one who thought of everything. Not only had he stocked his Lear with a splendid variety of liquor, liqueurs, wines and beers, he'd even provided an exceptionally attractive

61

stewardess to serve them up. All three men — Hamilton, Hiller and Serrano — had long, cold drinks in their hands. Hamilton gazed happily at the green immensity of the Amazonian rainforest passing by beneath them.

'This fairly beats hacking your way through that lot down there,' he said. He looked round the cabin of the luxuriously appointed jet. 'But this is for the carriage trade. What transport is Smith thinking of using when we make our trip into the Mato Grosso?'

'No idea,' Hiller said. 'Matters like that, Smith doesn't consult me. He's got his own advisers for that. You'll be seeing him in a couple of hours. I suppose he'll tell you then.'

'I don't think you quite understand,' Hamilton said in an almost gently explanatory tone. 'I only asked what transport he was *thinking* of using. Any decisions he and his experts have made are not really very relevant.'

Hiller looked at him in slow disbelief. '*You* are going to tell *him* what we're to use?'

Hamilton beckoned the stewardess, smiled and handed over his glass for a refill. 'Nothing like savouring the good life — while it lasts.' He turned to Hiller. 'Yes, that's the idea.'

'I can see,' Hiller said heavily, 'that you and

Smith are going to get along just fine.'

'Oh, I hope so, I hope so. You said we'd be seeing him in two hours. Could you make it three?' He looked disparagingly at his wrinkled khaki drills. 'These look well enough in Romono, but I have to see a tailor before I go calling on multi-millionaires. You say we're being met when we arrive. You think you can drop me off at the Grand?'

'Jesus!' Hiller was clearly taken aback. 'The Grand — *and* a tailor. That's expensive. How come? Last night in the bar you said you had no money.'

'I came into some later on.'

Hiller and Serrano exchanged very peculiar looks. Hamilton continued to gaze placidly out of the window.

★   ★   ★

As promised a car met them at the private airport in Brasilia. 'Car' was really too mundane a word to describe it. It was an enormous maroon Rolls-Royce, big enough, one would have thought, to accommodate a football team. In the back it had television, a bar and even an ice-maker. Up front — very far up front — were two uniformed men in dark green livery. One drove the car: the other's main function in life appeared to be

63

opening doors when the back seat — seats — passengers entered or left. The engine, predictably, was soundless. If it were part of Smith's pattern to awe visitors he most certainly succeeded in the case of Serrano. Hamilton appeared quite unimpressed, possibly because he was too busy inspecting the bar; Smith had somehow overlooked providing a stewardess for the rear of the Rolls.

They drove through the wide avenues of that futuristic city and pulled up outside the Grand Hotel. Hamilton dismounted — the door having magically been opened for him, of course — and passed swiftly through the revolving door. Once inside, he looked out through the glassed-in porch. The Rolls, already more than a hundred yards away, was turning a corner to the left. Hamilton waited until it had disappeared from sight, left by the revolving door by which he had entered and started to walk briskly back in the direction from which they had come. He gave the impression of one who knew the city, and he did: he knew Brasilia very well indeed.

★ ★ ★

Five minutes after dropping Hamilton the Rolls pulled up outside a photographer's shop. Hiller went inside, approached a smiling and affable assistant and handed over the film that had been taken from Hamilton.

'Have this developed and sent to Mr Joshua Smith, Haydn Villa.' There was no need for Hiller to add the word 'immediately'. Smith's name guaranteed immediacy. Hiller went on: 'No copy is to be made of this film and neither the person who develops it nor any other member of your staff is ever to discuss it. I hope that is clearly understood.'

'Yes, sir. Of course, sir.' The smile and the affability had vanished to be replaced by total obsequiousness. 'Speed and secrecy. Those are guaranteed, sir.'

'And a perfect print?'

'If the negative is perfect so will the print be.'

Hiller couldn't think of how else he could threaten the now thoroughly apprehensive assistant so he nodded and left.

★ ★ ★

Another ten minutes later and Hiller and Serrano were in the drawing-room of the Villa Haydn. Serrano was seated, as were Tracy, Maria and a fourth and as yet unidentified man. Smith talked somewhat apart with Hiller — 'somewhat apart' in that huge drawing-room meant a considerable distance

65

— glancing occasionally in Serrano's direction.

Hiller said: 'Of course, I can't vouch for him. But he knows an awful lot that we don't and I can always see to it that he'll make no trouble. Come to that, so would Hamilton. Hamilton has a rough way of dealing with people who step out of line.' Hiller went on to tell the sad tale of Serrano's mugging.

'Well, if you say so, Hiller.' Smith sounded doubtful and if there was one thing Smith didn't like it was being doubtful about anything. 'You certainly haven't let me down so far.' He paused. 'But your friend Serrano seems to have no history, no past.'

'Neither have most men in the Mato Grosso. Usually for the simple reason that they have *too* much of a past. But he knows his jungle — and he knows more Indian dialects than any man except maybe Hamilton. Certainly more than any man in the Indian Protection Service.'

'All right.' Smith had made up his mind and seemed relieved for that. 'And he's been close to the Lost City. Could be a useful back-up man.'

Hiller nodded towards the unidentified person, a tall, very heavily built, darkly handsome man in his mid-thirties.

'Who's that, Mr Smith?'

66

'Heffner. My chief staff photographer.'

Hiller said: 'Mr Smith!'

'Hamilton would think it extremely strange if I didn't take a staff photographer along on this historic trip,' Smith said reasonably. He smiled slightly. 'I will confess, though, that he can use one or two instruments other than his cameras.'

'I'll bet he can.' Hiller looked at Heffner with even closer interest. 'Another with or without a past?'

Smith smiled again but made no answer. A phone rang. Tracy, who was nearest to it, picked it up, listened briefly and replaced the receiver.

'Well, well. Surprise, surprise. The Grand Hotel has no one registered there under the name of Hamilton. Not only that, no member of the staff can recall ever seeing a man answering to the description.'

★　★　★

Hamilton, at that moment, was in a lavishly furnished suite in the Hotel Imperial.

Ramon and Navarro, seated on a couch, were admiring Hamilton, who was admiring himself in front of a full-length mirror.

'Always did fancy myself in a fawn seersucker,' Hamilton said complacently.

'Don't you agree? This should knock Smith for six.'

'I don't know about Smith,' Ramon said, 'but in that outfit you'd terrify even the Muscias. So no trouble with getting the invitation?'

'None. When he saw me flashing those gold coins in public he must have panicked in case someone else would step in fast. Now, I'm pleased to say, he's convinced he's got me hooked.'

'You still think that gold hoard exists?' Navarro said.

'I'm convinced it *did* exist. Not that it *does*.'

'Then why did you want those coins?'

'When this is over they will be returned and the money reimbursed — all except the two that are now in the possession of Curly, the head barman at the Hotel de Paris. But those were necessary: the shark, as we know, took the bait.'

'So, no hoard, huh?' Ramon said. 'Disappointing.'

'There is a hoard and a huge one. But not of those coins. Perhaps melted down, although that's unlikely. What is likely is that it's been split up into private collectors' hands. If you want to dispose of an art treasure, be it a stolen Tintoretto or a Penny

Black, then Brazil is *the* place in the world. The number of Brazilian millionaires who spend hours in their air-conditioned, humidity-controlled, burglar-proof deep underground cellars gloating over stolen Old Masters boggles the imagination. Ramon, there's a wet bar right behind you, and I'm developing a sore and thirsty throat from lecturing callow youngsters on the facts of criminal life.'

Ramon grinned, rose and brought a large whisky and soda to Hamilton and a soda each for himself and his brother — the twins never drank anything stronger.

Having eased his throat, Hamilton said: 'What did you get on Smith?'

'Nothing more than you expected,' Ramon said. 'The number of companies he controls is beyond counting. He's a financial genius, charming and courteous, totally ruthless in his business dealings and must by any reckoning be the richest man in the Southern hemisphere. A sort of Howard Hughes in reverse. About Hughes's early days everything was known in detail but the latter part of his life was so wrapped in mystery that many people who should have been in a position to know could scarcely believe that he had died on that flight from Mexico to the States, having been firmly convinced that he had died many years previously. Smith? Dead opposite. His past is a closed book and he never talks about it: neither do any of his colleagues, friends or supposed intimates — no-one really knows whether he *has* any intimates — for the good reason that none of them was around in his early days. Today, his life is an open book. He conceals nothing and operates in a totally straightforward fashion. Any one of the shareholders in his forty-odd companies can inspect the firm's books whenever they wish. He appears to have absolutely nothing to hide and I would suppose when you are as brilliant as he unquestionably is there's just no point in being dishonest. After all, what's the point in it if you can make more money being honest? Today he knows everybody's business and lets anyone who wishes know all about his businesses.'

'He's got something to hide,' Hamilton said. 'I know he has.'

Navarro said: 'What?'

'That's what we're going to find out, isn't it?' Hamilton said.

'I wish you wouldn't play your cards so close to your chest,' Navarro said.

'What cards?'

'We look forward to watching you at work, Mr Hamilton,' Ramon said. His tone was neutral to the point of being ambiguous. 'It should be worth watching. By every account, the man is totally above suspicion. He goes everywhere, sees everyone, knows everyone. And everyone knows that he and the President are blood brothers.'

★   ★   ★

The President's blood brother was leaning forward in a chair in his splendid drawing-room, oblivious of the company around him, staring in fascination at the silver screen. The room had been so efficiently darkened by the heavy drapes that he would have had difficulty in seeing those around him: had it been broad daylight, he still wouldn't have seen them. His absorption was total.

The transparencies were of superb quality, taken with a superb camera by an expert photographer who knew precisely what he was about. The colour was true, the clarity and the resolution impeccable. And the projector the best that Smith's money could buy.

The first group showed a ruined and ancient city, impossibly clinging to the top of a narrow plateau with, at the far end, a breathtakingly well-preserved ziggurat, as imposing as the best surviving works of the Aztecs or the Maya.

A second group showed one side of the city perched on the edge of a cliff that dropped vertically to a river and the rainforest beyond. The third group showed the other side of the city overlooking a similar gorge with a river sliding swiftly past in the distant depths. A fourth group, clearly taken from the top of the hills, showed a reverse view of the ancient city, with a brief glimpse of scrub-land beyond — once obviously terraced for cultivation — and with the two cliff-sides meeting in the middle distance. A fifth group, obviously taken 180° from the same position, showed a flat, grassy plateau, the sides curving to meet like the bows of a boat. Nearly incredible as those pictures were, the next few groups were staggering.

They were taken from the air and as transparency succeeded transparency, it became evident that they, like a number of the previous ones, could only have been taken from a helicopter.

The first of those helicopter shots showed the entire ruined city from above. The second, from perhaps five hundred feet higher up, showed that the city was perched on top of a vertically-sided, boat-shaped pinnacle of rock splitting a river which swept by on either side of it. Both arms of the river were rock-strewn, foaming white and clearly unnavigable. The third and fourth groups, from an even higher altitude, were a shock: taken horizontally they showed pictures of a densely crowded rainforest, reaching out, it seemed, almost to touch the camera and extending, unbroken, to the distant horizon. The fifth set, vertically downwards, made it clear that the great outer cliff-walls of the twin gorges were at least several hundred feet higher than the top of the cliff-walls that formed the island on which the Lost City was built. The sixth group, taken at a still higher elevation, showed just a narrow gap between two great stretches of forest reaching towards each other, with the Lost City just vaguely visible in the gloomy depths below. The seventh and last group, taken anywhere between five hundred and a thousand feet higher up again, revealed nothing but the continuous majestic sweep of the Amazonian rainforest, unbroken from pictorial horizon to pictorial horizon.

It was small wonder, then, that the planes of the Brazilian ordnance survey services, whose pilots claimed, probably rightly, to have criss-crossed every square mile of the Mato Grosso, had never discovered the site of the Lost City. It just could not be seen from the air. But the ancients had stumbled across it, discovered the most invisible, the most inaccessible, the most impregnable fortress ever created by nature or devised by man.

The viewers in the Villa Haydn drawing-room had sat throughout in silence. They knew they had seen something that no white man, with the exception of Hamilton and his helicopter pilot, had ever seen before, something, perhaps, that no-one had ever seen for generations, maybe even for centuries. They were hard people, tough people, cynical people, people who counted value only in the terms of cost, people conditioned to disbelieve, almost automatically, the evidence of their own eyes: but there is yet to be born a man or woman the atavistic depths of whose soul cannot be touched by that one questing finger that will not be denied, that primitive ancestral awe inseparable from watching the veil of unsuspected history being swept aside.

The slowly comprehending silence stretched out for at least a minute. Then, almost inaudibly, Smith exhaled his breath in a long sigh.

'Son-of-a-gun,' he whispered. 'Son-of-a-gun. He found it.'

'If your intention was to impress us,' Maria said, 'you've succeeded. What on earth was that? And *where* is it?'

'The Lost City.' Smith spoke absently. 'Brazil. In the Mato Grosso.'

'The *Brazilians* built pyramids?'

'Not that I know of. May have been some other race. Anyway, they're not pyramids, they're — Tracy, this is more in your field.'

'Well. Not really my field either. One of our magazines had an article on those so-called pyramids and I spent a couple of days with the writer and photographer on the job. Curiosity only, and wasted curiosity — I didn't learn much. Pyramid-shaped, sure, but those stepped-sided and flat-topped structures are called ziggurats. No-one knows where they originated although it is known that the Assyrians and Babylonians had them. Oddly enough, this style bypassed the virtually neighbouring country of Egypt, which went in for the smooth-sided and conically-topped version, but turned up again in ancient Mexico where some are still to be seen. Archaeologists and such-like use this as a powerful argument of prehistoric contact between east and west but the only sure fact is that their origins are lost in the mists of those same prehistoric times. My word, Mr Smith, this is going to drive those poor archaeologists up the wall. A ziggurat in the Mato Grosso.'

* * *

75

'Ricardo?' Hamilton said. 'I shall be leaving our friend's place in about two hours' time. I'll be driving — moment.' He broke off and turned to Ramon lounging on the couch in the Imperial Suite. 'Ramon, what shall I be driving?'

'Black Cadillac.'

'A black Cadillac,' Hamilton said into the phone. 'I do not wish to be followed. Thank you.'

3

There were six people in Smith's drawing-room that sunny afternoon — Smith himself, Tracy, Maria, Hiller, Serrano and Hamilton. All had glasses in their hands.

'Another?' said Smith. His hand reached out to touch the button that would summon the butler.

Hamilton said: 'I'd rather talk.'

Smith raised an eyebrow in slight if genuine astonishment. Not only had he heard from Hiller of Hamilton's reputation as a hard drinker, but his slightest suggestion was usually treated as a royal command. He withdrew his hand from the buzzer.

'As you wish. So we are agreed on the purpose of our visit. I tell you, Hamilton, I have done many things in the past that have given me a great deal of pleasure, but I've never been so excited — '

Hamilton interrupted him, something no-one ever did to Smith. 'Let's get down to details.'

'By God, you *are* in a hurry. I'd have thought that after four years — '

'It's a lot longer than that. But even after only four years a man starts to become a little impatient.' He pointed towards Maria and Tracy. People never pointed in Smith's drawing-room. 'Who are they?'

'We all know your rough diamond reputation, Hamilton.' When Smith chose to use a cold tone he could do so most effectively. 'But there's no need to be rude.'

Hamilton shook his head. 'Not rude. Just a man, as you observed, in a hurry. I just like to check on the company I'm keeping. As you do.'

'As I do?' Again the eyebrow. 'My dear fellow, if you would kindly explain — '

'And that's another thing,' Hamilton said. That made it twice in thirty seconds that Smith had been interrupted, which must have constituted some sort of a record. 'I don't like being condescended to. I am not your dear fellow. I am not, as you may come to learn, anybody's dear fellow. As you do, I said. Check up. Or perhaps you don't know the identity of the person who rang the Grand Hotel to see if I was actually staying there?'

It was a guess, but in the circumstances a safe one, and the flickered glance between Smith and Tracy was all the confirmation Hamilton required. He nodded towards Tracy.

'See what I mean?' Hamilton said. 'That's the nosey bastard. Who is he?'

'You would insult my guests, Hamilton?' Smith's tone was now positively arctic.

I don't much care who I insult — or should I say 'whom'? He's still a nosey bastard. Another thing, when I ask questions about people I do it honestly and in the open, not behind their backs. Who is he?'

'Tracy,' Smith said stiffly, 'is the managing director of McCormick-Mackenzie International Publications Division.' Hamilton looked unimpressed. 'Maria is my confidential secretary and, I might add, a close personal friend.'

Hamilton looked away from Tracy and Maria almost as if he had already dismissed them from his mind as being of no importance. 'I'm not interested in your relationships. My fee.'

Smith was obviously taken aback. Gentlemen did not discuss business negotiations in this crude and abrupt fashion. Momentarily, his expression hovered between astonishment and anger. Many years had passed since any man had dared talk to him in such a way. He required considerable willpower to repress his anger.

'Hiller mentioned it, I think,' Smith said. 'A six-figure sum. One hundred thousand dollars — U.S. dollars — friend.'

'I'm not your friend. A quarter million.'

'Ludicrous.'

'I could say 'Thanks for the drink' and walk out. I'm not childish. I hope you're not either.'

Smith had not become the man he was without the ability to make his mind up very rapidly indeed. Without in any way appearing to capitulate he capitulated immediately.

'A man would want an awful lot of service for money like that.'

'Let's get our terms clear. You get co-operation, not service. I'll return to this point later. I regard my fee as being far from excessive in view of the fact that I'm damned certain you're in this not just to get a few nice photographs and a human interest story. Who ever heard of Joshua Smith engaging upon any enterprise where money was not the prime and motivating factor?'

'As far as the past is concerned I would agree with you.' Smith's voice was quiet. 'In this particular instance money is not the principal factor.'

Hamilton nodded in acknowledgment. 'That could well be. In this particular instance I could well believe you.' Smith looked taken aback at Hamilton's concession, then his expression changed to one of speculation. Hamilton smiled. 'You're doubtless trying to figure out what I've figured out as the other motivation. You need not concern yourself for that in no way concerns me. Now, transportation?'

'What? What was that?' Smith had been caught off-balance by the sudden switch in topic which he should not have been as it was a favourite tactic of his own. 'Ah! Transportation.'

'Yes. What kind of transportation — air and water, we can forget land — do your companies have available?'

'A great deal, as you can imagine. What we don't have we can hire although I should think the need would be unlikely. Tracy has all the details. Tracy, by the way, is both a qualified pilot and helicopter pilot.'

'Helps. Where are the details?'

'Tracy has the details.' Smith said this in such a way as to convey the impression that he was not the man to be concerned with details, which was probably quite an accurate impression for he was famous for his gift in picking top-flight lieutenants and delegating the bulk of the executive work to them. Tracy, who had been following the conversation closely, rose, crossed to where they were standing and handed Hamilton a folder. The expression on Tracy's face bespoke a marked lack of affection: managing directors do not take kindly to being called nosey bastards. Hamilton appeared to notice nothing amiss.

He took the folder, read rapidly through the loose-leaf contents, pausing briefly now and again as something in particular caught his attention, then closed the folder. One could have been forgiven for assuming that Hamilton had already absorbed the contents: he probably had. For once, Hamilton seemed fairly impressed.

'Quite an air/sea fleet, haven't you? Everything from a Boeing 727 to a Piper Comanche. Double rotor freight helicopter — this is a Sikorsky Skycrane?'

'Yes.'

'And a hovercraft. Can the helicopter lift the hovercraft?'

'Naturally. That's why it was bought.'

'Where's the hovercraft? Corrientes?'

Smith said: 'How the devil do you know?'

'Logic. Wouldn't be much good to you here or in Rio, would it? I'll take this folder. See you this evening.'

'This evening?' Smith looked unhappy. 'Damn it, man, we have to draw up our plans and — '

'I'll draw up the plans. I'll explain them when I return with my assistants this evening.'

'Damn it all, Hamilton, *I* am putting up all the money. The man who pays the piper calls the tune.'

'This time out, you're second fiddle.'

Hamilton left, leaving behind him a brief but profound silence. Tracy said: 'Well. Of all the arrogant, hard-nosed, intransigent bastards — '

'Agreed, agreed,' Smith said. 'But he holds the cards, all of them.' He looked thoughtful. 'Enigma. Rough, tough, but dresses well, speaks well, obviously at home in any territory. Nuances, clever nuances. At ease in my drawing-room. Not many strangers are. Come to that, nobody is.'

Tracy said: 'And he's come to the conclusion that this Lost City is so dangerously inaccessible that he's not prepared to try the same route again. So — a helicopter. Or hovercraft.'

'I wonder.' Smith was still looking thoughtful. 'Why else would a man like that throw in his lot with us?'

'Because he's convinced he can eat us alive,' Maria said. She paused. 'Maybe he will at that.'

Smith looked at her without expression then crossed to the dining-room window. Hamilton was just moving away in his black Cadillac. A chauffeur stopped polishing a nondescript Ford, glanced towards Smith's window, nodded, climbed into his car and followed the Cadillac.

Hamilton was driving down one of

Brasilia's broad boulevards. He consulted his rear mirror. The Ford was about two hundred yards behind. Hamilton increased his speed. So did the Ford. Both cars were now travelling well above the speed limit. A police car appeared behind the Ford, switched on the siren, overtook and flagged the Ford to a stop.

★ ★ ★

The Ministry of Justice was a rather splendid building and the large airy office in which Hamilton sat across a polished leather table from Colonel Ricardo Diaz was suitably sumptuous. Diaz, in an immaculately cut uniform, was large, tanned and looked competent to a degree, which indeed he was. Diaz took a sip of some indeterminate liquid and sighed.

'About Smith, Mr Hamilton, you know as much as we do — everything and nothing. His past is a mystery, his present an open book that anyone is welcome to read. The dividing line between the present and the past can't be precisely delineated but it is known that he appeared — or, rather, emerged or surfaced in Santa Catharina, a province with a traditionally heavy Germanic settlement, in the late forties. Whether he is of similar origin is not known: his English is as immaculate as his Portuguese but, as far as is known, he has never been heard to speak German.

'His first business venture was to produce a newspaper aimed primarily at the native German speakers in the province but printed in Portuguese: it was conservative and strongly pro-establishment and marked the beginning of a long and close association with the government of the time, an association that has persisted, despite changes of government, until this day.

'He then branched out into the fields of early plastics and early ball-point pens. Smith was never an innovator — he was and remains a takeover specialist and a share manipulator of genius. Both the publishing and the industrial sides of his businesses expanded at a remarkable speed and within ten years he was, by any standards, a very wealthy man.'

Hamilton said: 'He couldn't have been without the odd cruzeiro to begin with.'

'Agreed. Expansion on a scale such as Smith's must have called for a great deal of capital.'

'And the source of capital is unknown?'

'Totally. But that's nothing to hold against any man. In this country — as in many others — we don't care to enquire too closely into those things.

'Now we come to Tracy. He is indeed the general manager of Smith's publication division. Very tough, very able, nothing known about him in the criminal line, which could mean that he's either honest or very clever. The best you can say of him is that he's a soldier of fortune. The police are certain that the bulk of his activities are illegal — diamonds have an odd habit of disappearing when he's in the neighbourhood — but he's never been arrested far less convicted. Serrano is a small-time crook, not too bright and a fearful coward.'

'He can't be all that cowardly if he ventures alone into the rainforests of the Mato Grosso. Not many white people would.'

'That thought, I admit, has also occurred to me. I'm merely passing on reported reputation, accuracy not guaranteed. Now, Heffner. Heffner's the joker. Wouldn't recognise a camera if he tripped over one. Well known to the New York police. Associated with crimes of violence and alleged gangland killings, but he's always beaten the rap. Not too surprising really — no police in any country are going to come over all zealous and excited when one hoodlum dispatches another. Curious fellow. Usually well spoken and civilised enough — look at those pillars of society, the Mafia bosses — but the veneer vanishes when he gets next to a bottle of bourbon. And he has a weakness for bourbon.'

'And all this leaves Smith unaffected?'

'Nothing known against him, as I said, but you can't associate with characters like Hiller, Heffner and Tracy without some tar rubbing off. Could well be the other way round, of course.' He looked up as a knock came at the door. 'Come in, come in.'

Ramon and Navarro entered. The twins were clad in khaki suits and smiling cheerfully. Diaz looked at them and winced.

'The famous Detective-Sergeant Herera and the famous Detective-Sergeant Herera. Or infamous. You are far from home, gentlemen.'

'Señor Hamilton's fault, sir.' Ramon spread his hands apologetically. 'He's always leading us astray.'

'Mary's little lambs. Ah. Major.'

A young officer entered and unrolled on the table a map of Southern Brazil. It was marked with legends of varying kinds. Differently coloured flags in circles and squares indicated different tribes, races and languages. Other symbols indicated the state of hostility or friendliness of the tribes.

The major said: 'This is the most up-to-date picture the Indian Protection

Service can give you. There are some places, you understand, where even the Service do not care to investigate too closely. Most of the tribes are friendly — pacified, if you like. Some are hostile. Nearly always the white man's fault. A very few cannibal tribes. Those are known.'

'And to be avoided, of course. The Chapates, Horenas and Muscias especially.'

Hamilton pointed at a town on the map and looked at Diaz. 'Corrientes. Smith has a hovercraft there — for obvious reasons. It's at the junction of the Paraná and Paraguay rivers and he must be pretty sure the Lost City lies near the head-waters of one of those. I'm going up the Paraguay. I don't know it well, there may be bad rapids for all I know, but the helicopter can help if there are.'

Diaz said: 'Your friend has a helicopter?'

'My friend, as you call him, has got everything. This is a giant — a Sikorsky Skycrane. Well enough named — it can just about lift any damn thing. We'll base the helicopter at Asunción. The hovercraft can go up in three stages — to either Puerto Casado or Puerto Sastre in Paraguay, then into Brazil to Corumbá then finally to Cuiabá. From there the helicopter can airlift it to Rio da Morte.'

'And you would like to have some units of the Federal army exercising near Cuiabá, is that it?'

'If it can be arranged.'

'That has already been done.'

'I am in your debt, Colonel Diaz.'

'It would be more accurate to say that we are in your debt. If, that is to say — '

'*If* I come back?'

'Precisely.'

Hamilton gestured towards the two young men. 'With the heavenly two to watch my back, what harm can befall me?'

Diaz looked at him briefly and doubtfully then pressed a button. An aide came in carrying a brown leather case, extracted what looked to be a large movie camera and handed it to Hamilton, who pressed a button on the base. There came the faint whirring noise typical of an electric-powered camera.

Diaz said: 'You won't believe this, but it will even take pictures if you wish.'

Hamilton smiled but without humour. 'I don't think I'll be indulging in any photography this time out. What's the radio transmitting range?'

'Five hundred kilometres.'

'Enough. Waterproof?'

'Naturally. You leave tomorrow?'

'No. We have to get provisions and jungle gear and fly them to Cuiabá. We must get the hovercraft on the move. More important, though, I must go ahead and check on our friend Mr Jones.'

'Back to the Colony?'

'Back to the Colony.'

Diaz said slowly: 'You are an extraordinarily persistent man, Mr Hamilton. God knows you've every right to be.' He shook his head. 'I greatly fear for the health of your travelling companions in your forthcoming expedition.'

*　*　*

Hamilton had rejoined his travelling companions-to-be. Outside the uncurtained windows of the Villa Haydn's drawing-room the sky was dark: the room itself was brightly but not harshly lit by the light from the three crystal chandeliers. There were nine people in the room, most of them standing, most of them with aperitif glasses in their hands. Present were Hamilton, the twin Sergeants Herera, Smith and his entourage. Heffner, to whom Hamilton had just been introduced, was slightly flushed of face, slightly loud of voice and was sitting on an arm of the chair Maria was occupying. Tracy was regarding him with disfavour.

Smith said to Hamilton: 'I must say your heavenly twins, as you call them, have an air of competence about them.'

'They're not much at home in drawing-rooms. But in the jungle, yes. They're good. Squirrel-hunter's eyes.'

'Meaning?'

'Either of them, with his rifle, can hit a playing-card at a hundred yards. Most people can't even see a card at that distance.'

'That meant to sound intimidating, threatening?'

'Neither. Reassuring. Very useful accomplishment when wild boars or alligators or head-hunters or cannibals come at you. Let's not confuse this coming trip with a Sunday school picnic.'

'I'm aware of that.' Smith was trying to sound patient. 'Well, your plan sounds reasonable. We leave in a couple of days?'

'More like a week. I repeat, no picnic: you don't go dashing off into the Amazonian rainforest at a couple of hours' notice, especially when you are going to be passing through hostile territory — and, believe me, we will be. We have to allow several days for the hovercraft to get up to Cuiabá — we don't know what difficulties it might encounter. Then we have to get all our provisions

91

and equipment and fly them over to Cuiabá. At least, you will. I have some business to attend to first.'

Smith raised an eyebrow. He was very good at raising eyebrows. 'What business?'

'Sorry.' Hamilton didn't sound sorry. 'Where can one hire a helicopter in this city?'

Smith took a deep breath then clearly made up his mind to ignore the outright rebuff. 'Well, you know I have this freight Sikorsky — '

'That lumbering giant? No thank you.'

'I have a smaller one. And a pilot.'

'Again, no thanks. Tracy's not the only one who can fly a helicopter.'

Smith looked at him in silence. His face was without expression but it was not difficult to guess what he was thinking: it would have been perfectly in keeping with Hamilton's secretive nature, his policy of never letting his left hand know what his right was doing, to have flown his own helicopter over the Lost City, so that no other person could share his knowledge. At last Smith said: 'Gracious, aren't you? You don't see a little friction arising when we set off on this search?'

Hamilton shrugged indifferently. 'It isn't a search. I know where I'm going. And if you think some friction is going to arise, then why don't you leave behind those liable to give rise to friction? It's a matter of indifference to me who comes along.'

'I'll decide that, Hamilton.'

'Will you, now?' Again the same indifferent, infuriating shrug. 'I don't think you've quite got the picture yet.'

It was significant of Smith's perturbation that he actually went to the bar and poured another drink for himself. Normally, indeed invariably, he would have summoned his butler to perform such menial tasks. He returned to Hamilton and said: 'Another point. You got your own way about making the plans — but we haven't yet decided who's going to be in charge of our little expedition, have we?'

'I have. I am.'

Smith's impassive air deserted him. He looked every inch the multi-billionaire he was reputed to be.

'I repeat, Hamilton, I'm the paymaster.'

'The ship-owner pays his captain. Who's in charge at sea? Even more importantly, who's in charge in the jungle? You wouldn't last a day without me.'

There was a sudden silence in the room. The tension between the two men was all too obvious. Heffner rose from the arm of the chair, lurched once and then crossed to where the two men were standing. The light of battle was in his truculent and bloodshot eyes.

'But, boss! You don't seem to understand.' Heffner didn't speak the words, he sneered them. 'This is the intrepid explorer himself. The one and only Hamilton. Haven't you heard? Hamilton is always in charge.'

Hamilton glanced briefly at Heffner then at Smith. 'This is the kind of irritant I mean. Born to give trouble, bound to give rise to friction. What function does he perform?'

'My chief staff photographer.'

'Looks the artistic type. He coming along?'

'Of course he is.' Smith's tone was glacial. 'Why on earth do you think Mr Tracy and I brought him down here?'

'I thought maybe he had to leave some place in a hurry.'

Heffner took a step closer. 'What does that mean, Hamilton?'

'Nothing, really. I just thought that maybe your friends in the New York police department were beginning to take too close an interest in you.'

Heffner was momentarily taken aback, then he took another menacing step forward. 'I don't know what the hell you mean. You wouldn't think of stopping me, would you, Hamilton?'

'Stopping you from coming along, dear me, no.'

Ramon looked at Navarro. Both men winced.

'Amazing,' Heffner said. 'All you require is twenty pounds over a man to make him see it your way.'

'Provided, of course, that you're half-way sober by that time.'

Heffner gazed at him in alcoholic disbelief then swung a roundhouse right at Hamilton's head. Hamilton moved inside it and brought up his own right in a wicked jab as Heffner's fist swept harmlessly by his head. Grey-faced and doubled over, Heffner sank to his knees, his hands clutching his midriff.

Ramon said thoughtfully: 'I do believe, Señor Hamilton, that he's half-way sober already.'

'A short way with mutineers, eh?' Smith was unmoved by the plight of his trusty chief photographer, and his irritation had given way to curiosity. 'You seem to know something about Heffner?'

'I read the occasional New York paper,' Hamilton said. 'Bit late when I get them, mind you, but that hardly matters as Heffner's activities cover a fair period. What the Americans call a scofflaw. Suspected involvement in various crimes of violence, even gangland killings. He's cleverer than he looks, which I don't believe, or he has a clever lawyer. Anyway, he's always beaten the rap so far. It is impossible, Mr Smith, that you had no inkling of this.'

'I confess that there have been stories, rumours. I discount them. Two things. He knows his job and a man is innocent until proved guilty.' Smith paused and went on: 'You know anything to my detriment?'

'Nothing. Everybody knows your life is an open book. A man in your position can't afford to have it otherwise.'

'Me?' said Tracy.

'I don't want to hurt your feelings but I never heard of you until today.'

Smith glanced down casually at a still prostrate Heffner, as if seeing him for the first time, and rang a bell. The butler entered. His face remained expressionless at the sight of the man on the floor: it was not difficult to imagine that he had seen such things before.

'Mr Heffner is unwell,' Smith said. 'Have him taken to his quarters. Dinner is ready?'

'Yes, sir.'

As they left the drawing-room Maria took Hamilton's arm. In a quiet voice she said: 'I wish you hadn't done that.'

'Don't tell me I've unwittingly clobbered your fiancé?'

'My fiancé! I can't stand him. But he has a long memory — and a bad reputation.'

Hamilton patted her hand. 'Next time I'll turn the other cheek.'

She snatched her hand away and walked quickly ahead of him.

★ ★ ★

Dinner over, Hamilton and the twins left in the black Cadillac. Navarro said admiringly: 'So now Heffner is labelled in their minds as your bad apple in the barrel while Smith, Tracy, Hiller and for all I know Serrano think that they are the driven snow. You really are a fearful liar, Señor Hamilton.'

'One really has to be modest about such things. As in all else practice makes perfect.'

4

As dusk approached, a helicopter, equipped
with both floats and skids, set down on a
sandy stretch on the left bank of the River
Paraná. Both up-river and down, on the same
bank, as far as the eye could see in the gloom,
stretched the dense and virtually impenetrable rainforest of the region. The far side of
the river, the right or western bank, was
invisible in the gathering gloom: at this point,
close to where the River Iquelmi flowed into
the Paraná, the parent river was more than
five miles wide.

The helicopter cabin was dimly lit even
although the precaution had been taken of
pulling black drapes across the windows.
Hamilton, Navarro and Ramon were having
their evening meal of cold meat, bread, beer
and soda — the beer for Hamilton, soda for
the twins.

Ramon shivered theatrically. 'I don't think I
much care for this place.'

'Not many people do,' Hamilton said. 'But
it suits Brown — alias Mr Jones — and his
friends well enough. Defensively speaking, it's
probably the most impregnable place in

South America. Years ago I traced Brown and his fellow-refugees to a place called San Carlos de Bariloche near Lake Ranco on the Argentine-Chilean border. God knows that was fortress enough, but he didn't feel secure even there so he moved to a hide-out in the Chilean Andes, then came here.'

Navarro said: 'He knew you were after him?'

'Yes. For years. Our wealthy friend in Brasilia has been after him for much, much longer. There may well be others.'

'And now he no longer feels secure even here?'

'I'm almost certain he doesn't. I know he was in the Lost City this year, and several times in the past few years. But he likes his comforts and there are none in that ruin. He may have taken a chance and returned. It's highly unlikely, but I have to check. Otherwise there's no point in going to the Lost City.'

'You have to have this confrontation between Brown and his friend.'

'Yes. I have no proof. This — ah — meeting will give me all the proof I ever require.'

'Remind me to take care of myself. I want to be alive to see it.' Navarro turned and gazed at the curtain facing downstream. 'It will not be easy to get into this place?'

'It will not be easy. Brown's estate here — it's known as Kolonie Waldner 555 — is better guarded than the Presidential Palace. The estate is hotching with trained killers as guards — and when I say that I mean they're trained and proven killers. There's dense jungle to the north and south — Paraguay lies to the south and Brown is a close friend of the President there — there's this river to the east and a large number of German settlements, populated almost exclusively by ex-members of the S.S., lie astride the roads to Asunción and Bella Vista. You won't even find a single river pilot here who is Brazilian born, they're all Germans from the River Elbe.'

Ramon said: 'In view of the fact of what you've just told us, a thought occurs to me. How do *we* get in?'

'I'll admit I've given the matter some thought myself. Not much option really. There's a road used by supply trucks, but it's too long, too dangerous and has to pass through an armed gatehouse with electrified fences stretching away on both sides. There's also a landing stage about ten miles downriver from here — about fifteen miles north of the Paraguayan border. The road up to the compound is about a mile long and usually heavily patrolled. But it's the only other way. At least there are no electrified fences along the right bank of the Paraná — or there weren't the last time I was there. We'll wait two hours and move on in.'

'Would it be in order,' Navarro said, 'if we gave you what is known as a couple of old-fashioned looks?'

'Help yourself,' Hamilton said agreeably. He opened a rucksack, brought out three silenced Lugers, three spare magazines and three sheathed hunting knives and distributed those. 'Sleep if you can. I'll watch.'

★　★　★

The helicopter, not under power, drifted with the current down the right bank of the Paraná, keeping as close inshore as possible to avoid the bright light of a brilliant half moon riding high in a cloudless sky. A door in the fuselage opened, a figure appeared, stepped down on to one of the pontoons and lowered an anchor quietly to the bed of the river. A second figure appeared with a bulky package under his arm: there came a subdued hiss and within thirty seconds a rubberised dinghy was fully inflated. A third man emerged from the fuselage carrying a small outboard motor and a medium-sized battery. The first two men stepped gingerly into the dinghy and took those items from him: the engine was clamped on to the transom aft, the battery lowered to the duckboard floor and coupled up to the engine.

The engine, once started, was almost soundless and the south-east wind, the prevailing one in that area, carried what little noise there was upstream. The painter was unhitched from the helicopter and the dinghy moved downstream. The three occupants were crouched forward, listening intently and peering, not without some apprehension, into the gloom beneath the overhanging branches of the rainforest trees.

A hundred yards ahead the river curved to the right. Hamilton switched off the electric motor, the twins dipped paddles into the water and very soon, a paddle occasionally touching the bank, they rounded the bend.

The landing stage, less than two hundred yards ahead, projected out into the river for a distance of twenty feet. Behind it, on land, there was a guardhouse which threw enough light to illuminate the cracked and splintered timber of the stage and two men, rifles shoulder-slung, maintaining a comfortable and relaxed guard on a couple of bent-wood chairs. Both were smoking and they were sharing a bottle. They stood up as two other men came out from the guardhouse. They talked briefly, then the two relieving guards took over their chairs — and the bottle — while the previous guards went inside the guardhouse.

The dinghy grounded silently on the muddy bank of the river and was secured by its painter to the low-hanging branch of a tree. The three men disembarked and disappeared into the undergrowth.

After they had gone about ten yards Hamilton said to Navarro in a barely audible whisper: 'What did I tell you? No electrified fences.'

'Watch out for the bear-traps.'

* * *

There were four men inside the guardhouse, all dressed in uniforms of the field-grey colour used by the Wehrmacht in the Second World War. Fully clad, they were lying on camp beds: three were asleep or appeared to be. The fourth was reading a magazine. Some instinct — there was certainly no sound — made him glance upwards and towards the doorway.

Ramon and Navarro were smiling benevolently at him. There was nothing particularly benevolent, however, about the discouragingly steady silenced Lugers held in their hands.

On the landing stage the two new guards

were gazing out over the Paraná when someone cleared his throat, almost apologetically, behind them. They immediately swung around. Hamilton wasn't even bothering to smile.

★　★　★

Inside the guardhouse all six guards were securely bound beyond any hope of escape and were more than adequately gagged. Ramon looked at the two telephones then questioningly at Hamilton, who nodded and said: 'No chances.'

Ramon sliced through the wires while Navarro started to collect the prisoners' rifles. He said to Hamilton: 'Still no chances?'

Hamilton nodded. The three men left, threw the rifles into the Paraná, then began to move up the road connecting the landing stage with Kolonie 555. The twins pressed in closely to the forest on the left-hand side of the road while Hamilton kept to the right. They moved slowly, with the stealth and silence of Indians: they had long moved at will through the disaffected tribes of the Mato Grosso.

When they were only yards from the compound Hamilton waved his two companions to a halt. The compound of the Kolonie was well lit by the moon. It was built in the basic form of a barrack square and was perhaps fifty yards across. Eight huts faced on to this central square. Most of those were extremely ramshackle, but one at the far left of the square was a solidly built bungalow. Close by that was an arched metal shed and, beyond that, a short runway. At the entrance to the compound, diagonally across the square from the bungalow, was a thatched hut which could well have been a guardhouse, a probability reinforced by the fact that a solitary figure leaned against the entrance wall. Like his colleagues on the landing stage he was in paramilitary uniform and carried a slung rifle.

Hamilton gestured to Ramon, who waved back. The three men vanished into the undergrowth.

The sentry, still leaning against the wall, had his head tilted back, a bottle to his lips. There came the sound of a muffled blow, the sentry's eyes turned up in his head and three disembodied hands appeared from apparently nowhere. One took the bottle from the already powerless hand while the other two took him under the armpits as he began to sag.

★ ★ ★

In what was indeed the guardhouse six more men lay trussed and gagged. Hamilton, alone in the middle of the room and engaged in rendering rifles and pistols inoperable, looked up as Ramon and Navarro, each with torch in hand, re-entered the room, shaking their heads. The three men left and began to move around the other huts. As they passed by each one, on each occasion Hamilton and Ramon remained outside while Navarro entered. Each time Navarro emerged, shaking his head. Finally, they arrived at the last building, the solidly constructed bungalow. All three entered. Hamilton, in the lead, found a switch and flooded the room with light.

It was a combination office and living quarters and furnished in considerable comfort. Drawers and filing cabinets were searched but they had nothing that interested Hamilton. They moved on to another apartment, a bedroom, and again a very comfortable place of accommodation. Pride of place on the walls were given to three framed and inscribed photographs — those of Hitler, Goebbels and Stroessner, a former Paraguayan president. The contents of the wardrobes were very sparse, indicating that the owner had removed the bulk of the contents. In one cupboard stood a pair of brown riding boots. The Nazis had always insisted on black riding boots, despising brown ones as being decadent: Stroessner, on the other hand, had favoured brown.

From there the three moved into what was Brown's communication centre, containing two large multicalibrated transceivers of the latest design. They located a tool-box and while Hamilton and Ramon used chisels and screwdrivers to remove the faceplates and destroy the inner mechanisms, Navarro located all the spares and reduced them too to scrap metal and shattered glass.

Navarro said: 'He's also got a very nice radio and transmitting set here.'

'You know what to do, don't you?'

Navarro knew what to do. From there they moved on to the arched metal shed. It was rather a remarkable place inasmuch as there ran down the middle of it what must have been the Kolonie's pride and joy, a genuine full-length American bowling alley. They paid no attention to this. What did attract their attention was a Piper Cub in a bay alongside the bowling alley. It took the men less than ten minutes to ensure that that particular Piper Cub would never fly again.

On their way back to the Paraná, this time walking openly in the middle of the road, Ramon said: 'So your friend *has* gone.'

'In that inelegant phrase, the bird has flown

the coop, taking most of his hard cases with him — Nazis, renegade Poles, renegade Ukrainians. As fine a collection of war criminals as you'll ever meet. This bunch here belongs strictly to the second division.'

'Where do you think they've gone?'

'We'll ask, shall we?'

The three men entered the landing stage guardhouse. Wordlessly, they sliced the ankle-bonds of one of the prisoners, removed his gag, dragged him to his feet and led him outside down to the river edge by the landing stage.

Hamilton said: 'Brown had three Piper Cubs. Where have the other two gone?'

The guard spat in contempt. At a signal from Hamilton, Navarro cut the back of the guard's hand. The blood flowed freely. The guard was then led forward until he was teetering on the very edge of the landing stage.

'Piranha,' Hamilton said, 'can smell blood at a quarter of a mile. Ninety seconds and you'll be white bones. If a crocodile doesn't get you first. Either way, being eaten to death is unpleasant.'

The guard looked in horror at his bleeding hand. He was trembling. 'North,' he said. 'North to Campo Grande.'

'And after that?'

'I swear to God — '

'Throw him in.'

'Planalto de Mato Grosso. That's all I know. I swear to you — '

Hamilton said wearily: 'Stop your damned swearing. I believe you. Brown would never entrust his secrets to vermin.'

Ramon said: 'What do we do with the prisoners?'

'Nothing.'

'But — '

'But nothing. I daresay someone will happen by and free them. Take this character inside and hobble and gag him.'

Navarro looked doubtful. 'It's a pretty deep cut. He could bleed to death.'

'Dear oh dear.'

5

Hamilton, Ramon and Navarro were in a taxi driving along one of Brasilia's broad boulevards. Ramon said: 'This woman, Maria, she comes?'

Hamilton looked at him and smiled. 'She comes.'

'There will be danger.'

'The more, the better. It will at least help to keep those clowns under control.'

Navarro was thoughtfully silent for a moment then he said: 'My brother and I hate all they stand for. But you, Señor Hamilton, hate so much more.'

'I have the reason. But I don't hate them.'

Ramon and Navarro looked at each other in lost comprehension then nodded as if in understanding.

★　★　★

A Rolls-Royce and a Cadillac had been backed out of Smith's six-car garage to make storage room for what Smith regarded as being more important, however temporarily, than the two cars. Hamilton, in the company

110

of the eight people who were going to accompany him, surveyed, with an apparently uncritical eye, the extremely comprehensive layout of the most modern and expensive equipments necessary for survival in the Amazonian rainforests. He took his time about it, so much so in fact that one or two of the watchers were beginning to look, if not apprehensive, then at least uncomfortable. Smith was not one of those. There was a slight tightening of the lips presumably indicative of a growing impatience. It was almost a law of nature that tycoons do not care to be kept waiting. Smith immediately proved that his patience was on a very short fuse indeed.

'Well, Hamilton? Well?'

'So. How the multi-millionaire — or is it billionaire? — travels into the boondocks. But good, really excellent.'

Smith visibly relaxed.

'But there's one exception, though.'

'Indeed?' One has to be very wealthy before one can — or is permitted to — raise one's eyebrows in the proper fashion. 'And what might that be?'

'Nothing missing, I assure you. Just some items surplus to requirements. Who are those guns and pistols for?'

'Us.'

'No deal. Ramon, Navarro and I carry weapons. You don't. None of you do.'

'We do.'

'Deal's off.'

'Why?'

'You are children in the rainforests. No popguns for kids.'

'But Hiller and Serrano — '

'I admit they know more than you do. That doesn't mean very much. In the Mato Grosso they might even rate as adolescents. Forget what they've ever told you.'

Smith lifted his shoulders, looked at the rather splendid armoury of weapons he had assembled, then back at Hamilton. 'Self-protection — '

'We'll protect you. I don't much fancy the prospect of you lot going around shooting harmless animals and innocent Indians. Even less do I fancy the prospect of being shot in the back when I've finally shown you where the Lost City is.'

Heffner stepped forward. He obviously had no doubt that the reference had been to himself. His fingers were actually clutching and unclutching, his face dusky with anger. 'Look here, Hamilton — '

'I'd rather not.'

'Stop it.' Smith's voice was cold and incisive but when he spoke again the tone had

112

changed to one of bitterness and left no doubt that he was addressing Hamilton. 'If I may say so, you have a splendid capacity for making friends.'

'Oddly enough, I do. I have quite a few in this city alone. But before I make a man my friend I have to make sure he's not my enemy or potential enemy. Very sensitive about those things, I am. But so's my back — sensitive, I mean, sensitive to having a knife stuck in it. I should know, I've had it done twice to me. I suppose I should have you all searched for flick-knives or some such toys but in your case I really don't think I'll bother. The harmless animals and innocent Indians are safe from any ill intentions you may develop, for, quite frankly, I can't see any of you lot taking on an armed Indian or a jaguar with what is, after all, little more than a pen-knife.' He made a small gesture with his right hand, as contemptuous as it was dismissive, and from the sudden tightening and whitening of Smith's lips, it occurred to Hamilton, not for the first time, that Smith might well and easily be the most dangerous man of them all.

Hamilton gestured again, this time towards the very considerable pile of equipment lying on the garage floor. 'How did those arrive — the packaging, I mean?'

'Crates. We crate them up again?'

'No. Too damned awkward to handle aboard a helicopter or hovercraft. I think — '

'Waterproof canvas bags.' He smiled at the slight surprise on Hamilton's face. 'We thought you might require something like that.' He pointed towards two large cardboard boxes. 'We bought them at the same time as we got the equipment. We're not mentally retarded, you know.'

'Fine. Your plane, a DC6, I understand — what's its state of readiness?'

'Superfluous question.'

'I suppose. Where are the hovercraft and helicopter?'

'Almost at Cuiabá.'

'Shall we join them?'

★　★　★

The DC6 parked at the end of the runway of Smith's private airfield may not have been in the first flush of youth but if the gleaming fuselage was anything to go by its condition would have ranked anywhere as immaculate. Hamilton, Ramon and Navarro, aided by an unexpectedly helpful Serrano, were supervising the loading of the cargo. It was a thorough, rigorous, painstaking supervision. Each canvas bag in turn was opened, its contents removed, examined, returned and

114

the bag then sealed to make it waterproof. It was a necessarily lengthy and time-consuming process and Smith's patience was eroding rapidly.

He said sourly: 'Don't take many chances, do you?'

Hamilton glanced at him briefly. 'How did you make your millions?'

Smith turned and clambered aboard the aircraft.

*   *   *

After half-an-hour's flying time out from Brasilia the passengers, with the exception of Hamilton, were all asleep or trying to sleep. No-one, it seemed, felt philosophical enough or relaxed enough to read: the clamour from the ancient engines was so great as to make conversation virtually impossible. Hamilton, as if prompted by some instinct, looked around and his gaze focused.

Heffner, sprawled in his seat, appeared, from his partly opened mouth and slow deep breathing, to be asleep, a probability lent credence by the fact that his white drill jacket, inadvertently unbuttoned, lay so as to reveal under his left armpit a white felt container which had obviously been designed to accommodate the aluminium flask inside.

This did not give concern to Hamilton: it was perfectly in character with the man. What did concern him was that on the other side of his chest could just be seen a small pearl-handled gun in a white felt under-arm holster.

Hamilton rose and made his way aft to the rear end of the compartment where the equipment, provisions and personal luggage were stored. It made for a very considerable pile, but Hamilton didn't have to rummage around to find what he was looking for — when loading he had made a mental note of where every item had been stored. He retrieved his rucksack, opened it, looked casually around to see that he was unobserved, removed a pistol and thrust it into an inside pocket of his bush jacket. He replaced the rucksack and resumed his seat up front.

*　*　*

The flight to Cuiabá airport had been uneventful and so now was the landing. The passengers disembarked and gazed around them in something like wonder, which was more than understandable as the contrast between Cuiabá and Brasilia was rather more than marked.

Maria was gazing around her in apparent disbelief. She said: 'So *this* is the jungle.

116

Quite, quite fascinating.'

'This is civilisation,' Hamilton said. He pointed to the east. 'The jungle lies over there. That's where we'll be very soon and once we get there perhaps you'd sell your soul to be back here.' He turned and said sharply to Heffner: 'Where do you think you're going?'

Heffner had been walking in the direction of the airport building. Now he stopped, turned and looked at Hamilton with a languid, insolent air.

'Talking to me?'

'I'm looking at you and I don't squint. Where are you going?'

'Look, I can't see it's any of your business, but I'm going to a bar. I'm thirsty. Any objections?'

'Every objection. We're all thirsty. But there's work to be done. I want all the equipment, food and luggage transferred to that DC3 there, and I want it done now. Two hours on and it will be too hot to work.'

Heffner glared at him, then looked at Smith, who shook his head. Sullenly, Heffner retraced his steps and approached Hamilton, his face heavy with anger. 'Next time I'll be ready, so don't be fooled by last time.'

Hamilton turned to Smith and said, almost wearily: 'He's your employee. Any more trouble or threats of trouble and he's on the DC6 back to Brasilia. If you disagree, I'm on the plane back there. Simple choice.'

Hamilton brushed contemptuously by Heffner who stared after him with clenched fists. Smith took Heffner by the arm and led him to one side, clearly having trouble keeping his anger in check. He said, low-voiced: 'Damned if I don't agree with Hamilton. Want to ruin everything? There's a time and a place to get tough and this is neither the time nor the place. Bear in mind that we're entirely dependent upon Hamilton. You understand?'

'Sorry, boss. It's just that the bastard is so damned arrogant. Pride cometh before a fall. My turn will come and the fall is going to be a mighty big one.'

Smith was almost kind. 'I don't think you quite understand. Hamilton regards you as a potential troublemaker — which, I have to say, you are — and he's the sort of man who will eliminate any potential source of trouble. God, man, can't you see? He's trying to provoke you so that he can have a reason, or at least an excuse, for disposing of you.'

'And how would he do that?'

'Having you sent back to Brasilia.'

'And failing that?'

'Don't even let us talk about such things.'

'I can take care of myself, Mr Smith.'

'Taking care of yourself is one thing. Taking care of Hamilton is another kettle of fish altogether.'

* * *

They watched, some of them with evident apprehension, as a giant twin-rotored helicopter, cables attached to four lifting bolts, clawed its way into the air, raising a small hovercraft with it. The hovercraft's rate of climb was barely perceptible. At five hundred feet, it slowly began to move due east.

Smith said uneasily: 'Those hills look mighty high to me. Sure they'll make it?'

'You'd better hope so. After all, they're your machines.' Hamilton shook his head. 'Do you think the pilot would have taken off unless he knew it was on the cards? Only three thousand feet. No trouble.'

'How far?'

'The headwaters of the Rio da Morte are only a hundred miles away. To reach the landing strip? Perhaps eighty. In half-an-hour's time we'll leave in the DC3. We'll still be there before them.'

Hamilton moved off and sat by the side of the river, idly lobbing stones into the dark waters. Some minutes later Maria appeared and stood uncertainly beside him. Hamilton looked up, smiled briefly, then glanced indifferently away.

She said: 'Is it safe to sit here?

'Boy-friend let you off the leash?'

'He's not my boy-friend.' She spoke with such vehemence that Hamilton looked at her quizzically.

'You could have fooled me. Misinterpretations, so easily come by. You have come, no doubt, or been sent, to ask a few craftily probing questions?'

She said quietly: 'Do you have to insult everybody? Wound everybody? Antagonise everybody? Provoke everybody? Back in Brasilia you said you had friends. It is difficult to understand how you came by them.'

Hamilton looked at her in some perplexity then smiled. 'Now look who's doing the insulting.'

'Between gratuitous insults and the plain truth there's a big difference. I'm sorry to have disturbed you.' She turned to walk away.

'Oh, come and sit down. Childish, childish. Maybe I can ask a few probing questions while you congratulate yourself on having found a chink in Hamilton's armour. I suppose that could be misinterpreted as an insult, too. Just sit down.'

She looked at him doubtfully. 'I asked if it's safe to sit here.'

'A damn sight safer than trying to cross a street in Brasilia.'

She sat down gingerly, a prudent two feet away from him. 'Things can creep up on you.'

'You've read the wrong books or talked to the wrong people. Who or what is going to creep up on us? Indians? There's not a hostile Indian within two hundred miles of here. Alligators, jaguars, snakes — they're a damned sight more anxious to avoid you than you are to avoid them. There are only two dangerous things in the forest — the *quiexada*, the wild boar, and the *carangageiros*. They attack on sight.'

'The caran what?'

'Giant spiders. Great hairy creatures the size of soup plates. They come at you one yard at a time. Jumping, I mean. One yard and that's it.'

'How horrible!'

'No problem. None in these parts. Besides, you didn't have to come.'

'Here we go again.' Maria shook her head. 'You really don't care much for us, do you?'

'A man has to be alone at times.'

'Evasion, evasion.' She shook her head again. 'You're always alone. Married?'

'No.'

'But you were.' It wasn't a question, it was a statement.

Hamilton looked at her, at the remarkable brown eyes which reminded him painfully of the only pair he'd ever seen like them. 'You can tell?'

'I can tell.'

'Well, yes.'

'Divorced?'

'No.'

'No? You mean — '

'Yes.'

'Oh! Oh, I am sorry. How — how did she die?'

'Come on. Plane to catch.'

'Please. What happened?'

'She was murdered.' Hamilton stared out across the river, wondering what had caused him to make this admission to a total stranger. Ramon and Navarro knew, but they were the only two in the world he'd told. Perhaps a minute passed before he became conscious of the light touch of finger-tips on his forearm. Hamilton turned to look at her and knew at once that she wasn't seeing him: the big brown eyes were masked in tears. Hamilton's first reaction was one of an almost bemused incomprehension: this was totally out of character with the image she — ably abetted by Smith — projected of

122

herself as a worldly-wise, street-wise cosmo-politan.

Hamilton gently touched the back of her hand and at first she didn't appear to notice. Perhaps half a minute passed before she wiped her eyes with the back of her free hand, disengaged her other hand, smiled apologeti-cally and said: 'I'm sorry. What must you think of me?'

'I think I may have misjudged you. I also think that in some way, some time, you may have suffered a lot.'

She had nothing to say to this, just wiped her eyes again, rose and turned away.

★ ★ ★

'Battered' is the adjective invariably, and perhaps inevitably, used to describe vintage and superannuated DC3s and this one was no exception: if anything it was an epitome, a prime example. The gleaming silver fuselage of yesteryear was but a fond and distant memory, the metal skin was pitted and scarred and appeared to be held together chiefly by large areas of rust: the engines, when started up, were a splendid comple-ment to the rest of the plane, coughing, spluttering and vibrating to such an extent that it seemed improbable that they would not be shaken free from the airframe. But the plane lived up to its reputation of being one of the toughest and most durable ever built. With what seemed a Herculean effort — it couldn't have been, it was under-loaded — it clambered off the runway and headed east into the late afternoon sky.

There were eleven people in the plane, Hamilton's party, the pilot and co-pilot. Heffner, as was customary, was taking counsel with a bottle of Scotch: the aluminium flask, presumably, was being held as an emergency reserve. Seated across the aisle from Hamilton, he turned to him and spoke or, rather, shouted, for the rackety clamour from the ancient engines was almost deafening.

'Wouldn't kill you to tell us your plans, would it, Hamilton?'

'No, it wouldn't kill me. But what does that matter? How's that going to help you?'

'Curiosity.'

'No secret. We land at Romono airstrip about the same time as the helicopter and hovercraft. Helicopter refuels — even those big birds have only a limited range — takes the hovercraft downstream, leaves it, returns and takes us down to join it in the morning.'

Smith, sitting in the seat next to Hamilton and listening, put a cupped hand to

Hamilton's ear and said: 'How far down-stream and why?'

'I'd say about sixty miles. There are falls about fifty miles from Romono. Not even a hovercraft could negotiate them so this is the only way we can get it past there.'

Heffner said: 'Do you have a map?'

'As it happens, I have. Not that I require it. Why do you ask?'

'If anything happens to you it would be nice to know where we are.'

'You better pray nothing happens to me. Without me, you're finished.'

Smith said into Hamilton's ear: 'You have to antagonise him? You have to be so arrogant? You have to provoke him?'

Hamilton looked at him, his face cold. 'I don't have to. But it's a pleasure.'

★   ★   ★

Romono airstrip, like Romono itself, looked, as it always did, a miasmic horror. The DC3 and the helicopter-cum-hovercraft arrived on the strip within minutes of each other. The helicopter's rotors had hardly stopped when a small fuel tanker moved out towards it.

The passengers disembarked from the DC3 and looked around them. Their expressions ranged from the incredulous to the appalled.

Smith contented himself with saying merely: 'Good God!'

'I don't believe it,' Heffner said. 'What a stinking, nauseating dump. Jesus, Hamilton, is this the best you could do for us?'

'What are you complaining about?' Hamilton pointed to the tin shed which constituted both the arrival and departure terminals. 'Look at that sign there. Romono International Airport. What more reassuring than that? This time tomorrow, gentlemen, you may well be thinking of this as home sweet home. Enjoy it. Think of it as the last outpost of civilisation. Look, as the poet says, your last on all things lovely every hour. Take what you need for the night. We have a splendid hotel here — the Hotel de Paris. Those who don't fancy it — well, I'm sure Hiller will put you up.' He paused. 'On second thoughts, I think I could have a better use for Hiller.'

Smith said: 'What kind of use?'

'With your permission, of course. You know that this hovercraft is the lynchpin to everything?'

'I'm not a fool.'

'The hovercraft will be anchored tonight in very dicey waters indeed. By which I mean that the natives on either side of the Rio da

126

Morte range from the unreliable to the downright hostile. So, it must be guarded. I suggest that this is not a task for one man, Kellner, the pilot, to do. In fact, I'm not suggesting, I'm telling you. Even if a man could keep awake all night, it would still be extremely difficult. So, another guard. I suggest Hiller.' He turned to Hiller. 'How are you with automatic weapons?'

'Can find my way around, I guess.'

'Fine.' He turned back to Smith. 'You'll find a bus waiting outside the terminal.' He reboarded the plane and emerged two minutes later bearing two automatic weapons and some drums of ammunition. By this time Hiller was alone. 'Let's go to the hovercraft.'

Kellner, the hovercraft pilot, was standing by his craft. He was thirtyish, sun-tanned, tough.

Hamilton said: 'When you anchor tonight don't forget to do so in midstream.'

'There'll be a reason for that?' Kellner, clearly, was an Irishman.

'Because if you tie up to either bank the chances are good that you'll wake up with your throat cut. Only, of course, you don't wake up.'

'I don't think I'd like that.' Kellner didn't seem unduly perturbed. 'Midstream for me.'

'Even there you won't necessarily be safe.

127

That's why Hiller is coming with you — needs two men to guard against an attack from both sides. And that's why we have those two nasty little Israeli sub-machines along.'

'I see.' Kellner paused. 'I'm not much sure that I care for killing helpless Indians.'

'When those same helpless Indians puncture your hide with a few dozen darts and arrowheads, all suitably or perhaps even lethally poisoned, you might change your mind.'

'I've already changed it.'

'Know anything about guns?'

'I was in the S.A.S. If that means anything to you.'

'It means a great deal to me.' The S.A.S. was Britain's elite commando regiment. 'Well, that saves me explaining those little toys to you, I suppose.'

'I know them.'

'One of my luckier days,' Hamilton said. 'Well, see you both tomorrow.'

* * *

The saloon of the Hotel de Paris, after closing hours, had six occupants. Heffner, glass in hand, was slumped in a chair, but his eyes were open: Hamilton, Ramon, Navarro,

Serrano and Tracy were asleep or apparently so, stretched out on benches or on the floor. Bedrooms were, that night, at a premium in the Hotel de Paris. As they were all equally dreadful and bug-ridden, Hamilton had explained, this was not a matter for excessive regret.

Heffner stirred, stooped, removed his boots, rose and padded his noiseless way across to the bar, deposited his glass on the counter, then crossed silently to the nearest rucksack. It was, inevitably, Hamilton's. Heffner opened it, searched briefly, removed a map, and studied it intently for some minutes before returning it to the rucksack. He returned to the bar, poured himself a generous measure of the Hotel de Paris's Scotch. Wherever the birthplace of that particular brand was it hadn't been among the highlands and islands of Scotland. He returned to his seat, replaced his shoes, leaned back in his chair to enjoy his nightcap, spluttered and emptied half the contents on the floor.

Hamilton, Ramon and Navarro, heads propped on hands, were regarding him with a quietly speculative air.

Hamilton said: 'Well, did you find what you were looking for?'

Heffner didn't say whether he had or not.

'One of the three of us is going to keep an eye on you for the remainder of the night. You try to stir from that chair and I will take the greatest pleasure in clobbering you. I don't much care for people who meddle in my private belongings.'

Hamilton and the twins slept soundly throughout the night. Heffner did not once leave his chair.

6

Just after dawn, the helicopter pilot, John Silver — generally known as Long John — was at the controls. The party of nine embarked and stowed their overnight luggage with the food and equipment that had been transferred from the DC3. Hamilton took the co-pilot's seat. So cavernous was the interior of the giant helicopter that it seemed virtually empty. It rose effortlessly and flew more or less east, paralleling the course of the Rio da Morte. All the passengers had their heads craned, peering through what few windows there were: they were seeing for the first time the true Amazonian rainforest.

Hamilton turned in his seat and pointed forward. 'That's an interesting sight.' His voice was a shout.

On a wide mud flat, perhaps almost a mile long, and on the left bank, scores of alligators lay motionless as if asleep.

'Good God!' It was Smith. 'Good God! Are there so many 'gators in the world?' He shouted to Silver: 'Take her down, man, take her down!' Then to Heffner: 'Your camera! Quick!' He paused, as if in sudden thought, then turned to Hamilton. 'Or should I have asked the expedition commander's permission?'

Hamilton shrugged. 'What's five minutes?'

The helicopter came down over the river in great sweeping, controlled circles. Long John was clearly a first-rate pilot.

The alligators, hemmed in the narrow strip between forest and river, seemed to stretch as far as the eye could see. It was, depending upon one's point of view, a fascinating, horrifying or terrifying spectacle.

Tracy said, almost in awe: 'My word, I wouldn't care to crash-land amongst that lot.'

Hamilton looked at him. 'Believe me, that's the least of the dangers down there.'

'The least?'

'This is the heart of the Chapate territory.'

'That meant to mean something to me?'

'You have a short memory. I've mentioned them before. It would mean something to you if you ended up in one of their cooking-pots.'

Smith looked at him doubtfully, clearly not knowing whether to believe him or not, then turned to the pilot.

'That's low enough, Silver.' He twisted in his seat and shouted at the top of his voice: 'God's sake, man, hurry!'

'Moment, moment,' Heffner bawled back.

'There's such a damned jumble of equipment here.'

There was, in fact, no jumble whatsoever. Heffner had already found his own camera, which lay at his feet. In Hamilton's rucksack he had found something that he had missed the previous night for the good enough reason that he hadn't been looking for it. He held a leather-bound case in his hand, the one Colonel Diaz had given to Hamilton. He extracted the camera from the case, looked at it in some puzzlement, then pressed a switch in the side. A flap fell down, noiselessly, on oiled hinges. His face registered at first bafflement, then understanding. The interior of the camera consisted of a beautifully made transistorised radio transceiver. Even more importantly it bore some embossed words in Portuguese. Heffner could read Portuguese. He read the words and his understanding deepened. The radio was the property of the Brazilian Defence Ministry, which made Hamilton a government agent. He clicked the flap in position.

'Heffner!' Smith had twisted again in his seat. 'Heffner, if you — Heffner!'

Heffner, radio case in one hand and his pearl-handled pistol in the other, approached. His face was a smiling mask of vindictive triumph. He called out: 'Hamilton!'

Hamilton swung around, saw the wickedly smiling face, his own camera held high and the pearl-handled pistol and at once threw himself to the floor of the aisle, his gun coming clear of his bush jacket. Even so, despite the swiftness of Hamilton's movement, Heffner should have had no trouble in disposing of Hamilton, for he had the clear drop on him and his temporarily defenceless target was feet away. But Heffner had spent a long night of agony in the Hotel de Paris. As a consequence, his hand was less than steady, his reactions were impaired, his co-ordination considerably worse.

Heffner, his face contorted, fired twice. With the first came a cry of pain from the flight deck. With the second the helicopter gave a sudden lurch. Then Hamilton fired, just once, and a red rose bloomed in the centre of Heffner's forehead.

Hamilton took three quick steps up the aisle and had reached Heffner before anyone else had begun to move. He stooped over the dead man, retrieved the camera-radio case, checked that it was closed, then straightened. Smith appeared beside him, a badly shaken man, and stared down in horror at Heffner.

'Between the eyes, between the eyes.' Smith shook his head in total disbelief. 'Between the eyes. Christ, man, did you have to do that?'

'Three things,' Hamilton said. If he was upset, he had his distress well under control. 'I tried to wing him, and I'm a good shot, especially at four paces, but the helicopter lurched. He twice tried to kill me before I pulled the trigger. Third thing. I gave orders that no-one was to carry guns. As far as I'm concerned, he's dead by his own hand. God's sake, why did he pull a gun on me? Was he mad?'

Smith, perhaps fortunately, was given no time to lend consideration to either of those things, even had he then been of a mind to, which he almost certainly was not. The helicopter had given another and even more violent lurch, and although it still carried a good deal of forward momentum, seemed to be fluttering and falling from the sky like a wounded bird. It was a singularly unpleasant sensation.

Hamilton ran forward, clutching at whatever he could to maintain his balance. Silver, blood streaming from a cheek wound, was fighting to regain control of the uncontrollable helicopter.

Hamilton said: 'Quick! Can I help?'

'Help? No. I can't even help myself.'

'What's happened?'

'First shot burnt my face. Nothing. Superficial. Second shot must have gone through one or more hydraulic lines. Can't see exactly but it can't have been anything else. What happened back there?'

'Heffner. Had to shoot him. He tried to shoot me, but he got you and your controls instead.'

'No loss.' Considering the circumstances, Silver was remarkably phlegmatic. 'Heffner, I mean. This machine is a different matter altogether.'

Hamilton took a quick look backwards. The scene, understandably, was one of confusion and consternation although there were no signs of panic. Maria, Serrano and Tracy, all three with almost comically dazed expressions, were sitting or sprawling in the central aisle. The others clung desperately to their seats as the helicopter gyrated through the sky. Luggage, provisions and equipment were strewn everywhere.

Hamilton turned again and pressed his face close to the windscreen. The now pendulum-like motion of the craft was making the land below swing to and fro in a crazy fashion. The river was still directly beneath: the one plus factor appeared to be that they had now left behind them the mudflats where the alligators had lain in so lifeless a manner. Hamilton became suddenly aware that an island, perhaps two hundred yards long by half as wide, lay ahead of them in the precise middle of the river, at a distance of about half a mile: it was wooded but not heavily so. Hamilton turned to Silver.

'This thing float?'

'Like a stone.'

'See that island ahead?'

They were now less than two hundred feet above the broad brown waters of the river: the island was about a quarter of a mile ahead.

'I can see it,' Silver said. 'I can also see all those trees. Look, Hamilton, control is close to zero. I'll never get it down in one piece.'

Hamilton looked at him coldly. 'Never mind the damned chopper. Can you get *us* down in one piece?'

Silver glanced briefly at Hamilton, shrugged and said nothing.

The island was now two hundred yards distant. As a landing ground it looked increasingly discouraging. Apart from scattered trees it was, but for one tiny clearing, thickly covered with dense undergrowth. Even for a helicopter in perfect health it would have made an almost impossible landing site.

Even in that moment of emergency some instinct made Hamilton glance to the left. Directly opposite the island, at about fifty yards' distance and on the bank of the river, was a large native village. From the expression — or lack of it — on Hamilton's face it was clear that he didn't care for large native villages, or, at least, this particular one.

Silver's face, streaked with rivulets of sweat and blood, reflected a mixture of determination and desperation, with the former predominating. The passengers, tense, immobile, gripped fiercely at any available support and stared mutely ahead. They, too, could see what was about to happen.

The helicopter, swinging and side-slipping, weaved its unpredictable way towards the island. Silver was unable to bring the helicopter to the hover. As they approached this one much too small clearing, the helicopter was still going far too fast. Its ground-level clearance was by then no more than ten feet. The trees and undergrowth rushed at them with accelerating speed.

Silver said: 'No fire?'

'No fire.'

'No ignition.' Silver switched off.

One second later the helicopter dipped sharply, crashed into the undergrowth, slid about twenty feet and came to a jarring stop against the bole of a large tree.

For a few moments the silence was complete. The engine roar had vanished. It was a silence compounded of the dazed shock caused by the violence of their landing and the relief of finding themselves still alive. No-one appeared to have sustained any injury.

Hamilton reached out and touched Silver's arm. 'I'll bet you couldn't do that again.'

Silver dabbed at his wounded cheek. 'I wouldn't ever care to try.' If he was in any way proud of his magnificent airmanship it didn't show.

'Out! All out!' Smith's voice was a stentorian shout, he seemed unaware that normal conversational tones were again in order. 'We can go up any moment.'

'Don't be so silly.' Hamilton sounded weary. 'Ignition's off. Stay put.'

'If I want to go out — '

'Then that's your business. Nobody's going to stop you. Later on, we'll bury your boots.'

'What the hell is that meant to mean?'

'A civilised interment of the remains. Maybe even those won't be left.'

'If you'd be — '

'Look out your window.'

Smith looked at Hamilton then turned to the window, standing so as to achieve a ground view. His eyes widened, his lips parted and his complexion changed for the worse. Two very large alligators were only feet from the helicopter, fearsome jaws agape, their huge tails swinging ominously from side to side. Wordlessly, Smith sat down.

Hamilton said: 'I warned you before you left, the Mato Grosso is no place for mindless little children. Our two friends out there are just waiting for such children. And not only those two. There'll be more around, lots of them. Also snakes, tarantulas and suchlike. Not to mention — ' He broke off and pointed to the port windscreen. 'I'd rather you didn't have to but take a look anyway.'

They did as he asked. Among the trees on the left bank could be seen a number of huts, perhaps twenty in all, with an especially large circular one in the centre. Several columns of smoke shimmered up into the morning air. Canoes, and what looked like a pinnace, fronted the village. A large number of natives, nearly naked, stood on the bank, talking and gesticulating.

'But this is luck,' Smith said.

'You should have stayed in Brasilia.' Hamilton sounded unwontedly sour. 'Sure it's luck — the most fiendishly bad luck. I see the chiefs are getting ready.'

There was a fairly long silence then Maria said almost in a whisper: 'The Chapate?'

'None else. Complete, as you can now see, with olive branches and calling cards.'

Every native ashore was now armed or was in the process of getting armed. They carried spears, bows and arrows, blowpipes and machetes. The angry expressions on their faces went well with the menacing gesticulations in the direction of the island.

'They'll be calling soon,' Hamilton said, 'and not for tea. Maria, would you give Mr Silver a hand to fix up his face?'

Tracy said: 'But we're safe here, surely? We have guns, plenty. They're carrying nothing that could penetrate our screens, far less the fuselage.'

'True. Ramon, Navarro, get your rifles and come with me.'

Smith said: 'What are you going to do?'

'Discourage them. From crossing. Shame, really. They may not even know what a gun is.'

'Tracy made sense,' Smith said. 'We're safe here. You *have* to be a hero?'

Hamilton stared at him until Smith looked uncomfortable. Hamilton said: 'Heroism doesn't enter into it, just survival. I wonder whether *you* would be half-way brave enough to fight for your own survival. I suggest you leave this to someone who knows how the Chapate wage war. Or do you want to be ready for immediate consumption when they get you?'

'What's that supposed to mean?' Smith tried to sound blustery but his heart wasn't in it, his ego had been too severely dented.

'Just this. If they get as much as a foothold on this island the first thing they'll do is to set fire to the undergrowth and roast you alive in this metal coffin.'

There was a silence that lasted until Hamilton, Ramon and Navarro had left the helicopter.

Ramon, the first to touch the ground, had his rifle on the nearest alligator immediately but the precaution proved needless: both alligators immediately turned and scuttled away into the undergrowth.

Hamilton said: 'Just keep an eye on our backs, Ramon.' Ramon nodded. Hamilton and Navarro moved towards the rear, took shelter behind the tail of the helicopter and looked cautiously ashore.

A squat, powerfully built Indian dressed in a pink feather headdress, teeth necklace, a series of arm bracelets and little else — definitely the chief — was ordering warriors into half-a-dozen canoes. He himself was standing on the bank.

Navarro looked at Hamilton, his reluctance plain. He said: 'No choice?'

With equal regret Hamilton agreed, shaking his head. Navarro lifted his rifle, aimed and fired in one swift motion. The report of the rifle momentarily paralysed all activity on the bank. Only the chief moved: he cried out in pain and clutched his upper right arm. A second later, while the warriors were still immobilised in shock, another report was heard and another warrior struck in precisely the same place. Navarro was clearly a marksman of the most extraordinary accuracy.

Navarro said: 'Not nice, Señor Hamilton.'

'Not nice. As the old saying goes, it's people like us who have made people like them what they are. But this is hardly the time and place to explain that to them.'

Ashore the warriors rapidly abandoned their canoes and ran for the shelter of their huts and the forest, taking the two wounded men with them. From those shelters they could be seen almost immediately drawing bows and lifting blowpipes to their mouths. Hamilton and Navarro prudently dropped behind cover as arrows and darts rattled and rebounded harmlessly off the fuselage. Navarro shook his head in sorrow and wonderment. 'I'll bet they've never even *heard* a rifle report before. It is something less than a fair contest, Señor Hamilton.'

Hamilton nodded, but made no comment for comment would have been superfluous.

He said: 'That's all for now. I don't think they'll try anything again before dark. But I'll keep watch — or arrange for others to do it. Meantime, you and Ramon get rid of our four-legged friends and the creepy-crawlies. Try to chase them away, shoo them away. If you have to shoot, for goodness' sake don't do it by the water's edge or in the water. Bath-time tonight and I don't want to attract every piranha for miles around.'

Hamilton reboarded the helicopter. Tracy said: 'That was quite a hailstorm out there. Arrows and darts, I assume?'

'Didn't you see?'

'I wasn't too keen on looking. I'm sure those windows are made of toughened glass but I wasn't going to be the one to put them to the test. Poisoned?'

'Certainly. But, almost equally certainly, no curare, nothing lethal. They have a less final but equally effective poison that merely stuns. Too much curare affects the flavour of the stew.'

Smith said sourly: 'You certainly have a summary way of dealing with the opposition.'

'I should have parleyed with them? The brightly coloured beads approach? Why don't you go and try it?' Smith said nothing. 'If you have any futile suggestions to offer, I suggest you either translate them into action or shut up. There's a limit to the number of niggling remarks a man can take.'

Silver, his face bandaged, intervened pacifically. 'And now?'

'A lovely long siesta until dusk. For me, that is. I shall have to ask you to take turns in keeping watch. Not only the village, but as far upstream and downstream as you can see — the Chapate might contemplate launching a canoe attack at some distance from their village although I consider it highly unlikely. If anything happens, let me know. Ramon and Navarro should be back in twenty minutes; don't bother letting me know.'

Tracy said: 'You place a great deal of faith in your lieutenants.'

'Total.'

Smith said: 'So we keep awake while you sleep. Why?'

'Recharging my batteries for the night ahead.'

'And then?'

Hamilton sighed. 'This helicopter, obviously, will never be airborne again so we have to find some other means of rejoining the hovercraft, which I reckon must be about thirty miles downstream. We can't go by land. It would take us days to hack our way down there and, anyway, the Chapate would get us before we covered a mile. We need a boat. So we'll borrow one from the Chapate. There's a nice, big and very ancient motor launch moored to the bank there. Not their property for a certainty: the original owners were probably eaten long ago. And the engine will be a solid block of rust and quite useless. But we don't need power to go downstream.'

Tracy said: 'And how do you propose we — ah — obtain this boat, Mr Hamilton?'

'I'll get it. After sunset.' He smiled faintly. 'That's why I intend recharging my batteries in advance.'

Smith said: 'You really do have to be a hero, Hamilton, don't you?'

'And you'll really never learn, will you? No, I don't have to be a hero. I don't want to be a hero. You can go instead. You be the hero. Go on. Volunteer. Impress your girl-friend.'

Smith slowly unclenched his fists and turned away. Hamilton sat and appeared to compose himself for slumber, oblivious of the dead Heffner laid now across the aisle from him. The others looked at one another in silence.

★ ★ ★

It was many hours later, at dusk, when Hamilton said: 'Everything packed? Guns, ammunition, last night's overnight bags, food,

146

water, medicines. And, Silver, the chopper's two compasses might come in handy.'

Silver indicated a box by his feet. 'They're already in there.'

'Excellent.' Hamilton looked around him. 'Well, that seems to be all. Heigh-ho, I think.'

'What do you mean, that seems to be all?' Smith said. He nodded towards the dead Heffner. 'How about him?'

'Well, how about him?'

'You going to leave him here?'

'That's up to you.' Hamilton spoke with an almost massive indifference. He did not have to spell out his meaning. Smith turned and stumbled down the helicopter steps.

At the downstream end of the island, only Navarro, of all the party, was absent. In the gathering darkness Hamilton again checked all the various packs. He seemed satisfied.

'There will be a moon,' he said, 'but it will be too late to save us. Moonrise is in about two and a half hours. When they attack — there's no 'if' about it — it must be inside those two and a half hours, which means it could be any time now although I should guess that they'll wait a bit until it is as dark as possible. Ramon, join Navarro now. If they attack before you get my signal, hold them off as best you can for as long as you can. If my signal comes first, get back here at once. Tracy?'

Tracy said: 'I can tell you, I haven't been too happy here for the past hour. No, no alligators. No sign. Not a ripple. No gun?'

'Guns make noises. Guns get wet.'

Maria shivered and pointed to his big sheath knife. 'And that does neither?'

'Sometimes the first blow doesn't kill. Then there can be a lot of noise. But no heroics. I don't expect to have to use it. If I do, it means I've botched my job.'

Hamilton looked out across the river. The darkness had now so deepened that the shoreline was no more than a dimly seen blur. He checked that the coil of rope, the waterproof torch and the sheath knife were securely attached to his waist, walked noiselessly into the river and then slowly, silently, began to swim.

The water was warm, the current was gentle and around him he could see nothing but the calm dark water. Suddenly, he stopped swimming, trod water and stared ahead. He could see what he imagined to be a tiny ripple in the black smoothness without being able to see what caused it. His right hand came clear of the water, clenched round the haft of his sheath knife. The tiny ripple was still there but even as he strained to watch it, it disappeared. Hamilton replaced the knife in its sheath. He wasn't the first person to have mistaken a drifting log for a crocodile, a considerably healthier position than the other way round. He resumed his silent swimming.

A minute later he drifted in towards the bank and caught hold of a convenient tree root. He straightened, paused, looked carefully around, listened intently then emerged swiftly and silently from the river and disappeared into the forest.

A hundred yards brought him to the perimeter of the village. There were at least a score of native huts, haphazardly arranged, none of them showing any sign of life. In their approximate centre was the much larger circular hut: light could be seen through the numerous chinks in its walls. Ghostlike, Hamilton moved off to his right and moved round the perimeter of the village until he was directly to the rear of the large hut. Here he waited until he was sure — or as sure as he could possibly be — that he was alone then moved forward to the rear of the hut. He selected a small, lighted chink in the wall and peered through it.

The communal hut was illuminated by some scores of tallow tapers. It was completely unfurnished. Dozens of natives were standing several deep round a cleared space in the middle where an elderly man was using a stick to make a diagram on the sand-covered floor while at the same time explaining something in an unintelligible tongue. The diagram was the outline of the island. Also shown was the left bank of the river on which the village stood. The speaker had drawn lines from the village, from above the village and from below the village, all towards the island. A multi-pronged attack was to be launched on the helicopter and its passengers. The lecturer lifted his stick from time to time and pointed it at various natives: it was apparent that he was allocating canoe crews for their lines of attack.

Hamilton moved away in the direction of the upper river bank, still circling the village perimeter. As he passed the last hut, he stopped. At least twenty canoes, some quite large, were tethered to the bank. Almost at the end of the row, upriver, was the dilapidated, paintflaked motor launch, a little over twenty feet in length. It was deep in the water but floating so to that extent might be deemed riverworthy.

Two Indian warriors, talking quietly, stood guard at the downstream end of the row of canoes. As Hamilton watched, one of them gestured towards the village and walked away.

Hamilton moved around to one side of the hut and crouched there: the Indian walked by on the other side.

Another problem had arisen, one that Hamilton could well have done without. Even fifteen minutes ago he could have remained where he had been and the remaining Indian could have come within a few feet without seeing him. Not any more. The sun was gone, moonrise was still some time away, but, unfortunately, the evening clouds which, earlier, had so obligingly offered concealment, had passed away and the southern skies were alive with stars — and in the tropics stars always seem so much bigger and brighter than they do in temperate climes. Visibility had become disconcertingly good.

Hamilton knew that the last thing he could afford to do was to wait. He straightened and advanced soundlessly, knife held in the throwing position. The Indian was gazing out towards the island, now quite visible. A shadow appeared behind him and there came the sound of a sharp but solid blow as the haft of Hamilton's knife caught him on the base of the neck. Hamilton caught him as he was about to topple into the water and lowered him none too gently to the bank.

Hamilton ran upstream. He came to the motor launch, pulled out his signal torch, hooded the beam with his hand and shone it inside.

The launch was filthy and had at least four inches of water in the bottom. The torch beam lit on the centrally positioned engine which, as Hamilton had expected, was now no more than a solid block of rust. Floating incongruously in its vicinity were three cooking pans, obviously intended as bailers, at a guess the property of some optimistic but now departed missionaries. The beam played swiftly around the entire interior of the boat. There was no means of propulsion whatsoever: no mast, no sail, no oars, not even a solitary paddle.

Hamilton straightened and moved quickly to examine some of the nearest canoes. Within a minute he had collected at least a dozen paddles. He deposited those in the launch, hurried away, selected two large canoes and pulled them close to the launch. He unwound the rope around his waist, cut off two sections and used those to tie the canoes in tandem to the launch. He sliced through the manila painter, pushed the launch into deeper water, scrambled in, seized a paddle and began to move silently away from the bank.

Paddling the launch — and its attendant canoes — diagonally downstream, Hamilton was soon making heavy weather of it. The launch was naturally cumbersome and made more so by the amount of water in it and Hamilton, able to use only one paddle, had to switch continuously from side to side to keep it on course. Briefly, he paused, located what he could discern to be the upstream end of the island, now almost directly opposite him, pulled out his torch and pressed the button three times. He then pointed his torch diagonally downstream and flashed again three times. He replaced his torch and resumed paddling.

Ashore, an Indian warrior emerged from the communal hut, and walked casually towards the upper river bank. Suddenly, he hurried forward and stooped over an Indian lying face-down on the bank. A trickle of blood was coming from what was the beginning of a massive bruise on the base of his neck. His fellow tribesman straightened and began to shout, repeatedly and urgently.

Hamilton momentarily ceased paddling and glanced involuntarily over his shoulder. Then he bent himself again to his task but with even more energy this time.

Ramon and Navarro, as by pre-arrangement, had already begun to move to the other end of the island. Now they stopped abruptly when they heard the cry ashore, a cry now taken up by the shouting of many more angry voices.

Ramon said: 'I think Señor Hamilton must have been up to something. I also think we'd better wait a little.'

The two men crouched on the island shore, rifles at the ready, and peered out across the channel. The bulky outline of Hamilton's launch and the two canoes he was towing were now visible not thirty yards from where they were. Not as visible, but still distinct enough to be unmistakable, were the shadowy forms of canoes putting out from the village in pursuit.

Ramon shouted: 'As close to the island as you can. We'll cover you.'

Hamilton glanced over his shoulder. The nearest of half a dozen canoes was already less than thirty yards away. Two men stood in the bows, one with a blowpipe to his mouth, the other pulling back the string of his bow.

Hamilton crouched as low as possible in the boat, glancing almost desperately to his right. He could now see both Ramon and Navarro and he could see that they had their rifles levelled. The two shots came simultaneously. The warrior with the blowpipe toppled backwards in the canoe: the one with the drawn bow pitched into the water, his arrow hissing harmlessly into the river.

'Quickly,' Hamilton called. 'Join the others.'

Ramon and Navarro loosed off a few more shots, more for the sake of discouragement than with the intent of hitting anything, then began to run. Thirty seconds later they rejoined the remainder of the party at the downstream end of the island, all looking anxiously upriver. Hamilton was struggling, unsuccessfully, to bring his unwieldy trio of boats ashore: it looked as if he would miss the tip of the island by feet only.

Ramon and Navarro handed over their rifles, plunged into the river, seized the bows of the motor launch and turned it into the shore. There were no orders given, no shouts for haste: such were needless. Within seconds all the equipment and passengers were aboard the motor launch, the boat pushed off and paddles distributed. They cast frequent and apprehensive glances astern but there was no cause for concern. The canoes, unmistakably, were dropping behind. There was going to be no pursuit.

Smith said, not even grudgingly: 'That was rather well managed, Hamilton. And now?'

'First we bail out. There should be three cooking pans floating around somewhere. Then we move out into the middle of the river — just in case they've sent some

155

sharp-shooters down the left bank. There's going to be a full moon shortly, the skies are cloudless so we might as well carry on. Kellner and Hiller must be distinctly worried about us by this time.'

Tracy said: 'Why the two empty canoes?'

'I told you yesterday evening that there were falls about fifty miles below the town. That's why we had to airlift the hovercraft beyond them. The falls are about twenty miles farther on now. We'll have to make a portage there and it would be impossible to make it with this elephant. When we get there and have emptied her we'll give her a shove over the edge. Maybe she'll survive, the falls are only fifteen feet.'

Some little time later the now bailed-out motor launch glided gently down the centre of the river, six men at the paddles but not exerting themselves; the current bore them along. The newly risen moon gleamed softly on the brown water. It was a peaceful scene.

★ ★ ★

Five hours later, as Hamilton guided the launch into the left bank, the passengers could distinctly hear the sound of the falls ahead, no Niagara roar, but unmistakably falls. They made the bank and tied up to a

156

tree. The portage was not more than a hundred yards. First all the equipment, food and personal luggage were carried down, then the two canoes, and just in case the motor launch should survive its fall, the three cooking utensils for bailing as well.

Hamilton and Navarro climbed into a canoe and reached a spot where the white water ended about a hundred feet below the foot of the falls and paddled gently to maintain position. Both men were looking upriver towards the falls beyond which, they knew, Ramon was at work.

For half a minute there was only the brown-white smoothness of the Rio da Morte sliding vertically downwards. Then the bows of the motor launch came in sight, appeared to hesitate, until suddenly the entire boat was over and plunging down. There was a loud smack and a considerable cloud of spray as the launch first entered the water then disappeared entirely. All of ten seconds elapsed before it reappeared. But reappear it did, and, remarkably, right side up.

The launch, so full of water that there were only about four inches of freeboard left, drifted sluggishly downstream until Hamilton got a line aboard. With no little difficulty he and Navarro towed it to the left bank and tied up. Bailing operations commenced.

The brightly illuminated hovercraft lay anchored in midriver. Navigation, deck and cabin lights were on. Kellner and Hiller were already close to despair because the expected arrivals were already fifteen hours late and it hardly seemed likely that if they hadn't arrived by that time, that they would be arriving at all. They had no cause for worry as far as they themselves were concerned. They had only to continue downriver till they came to the junction with the Araguaia and some form of civilisation. Both men were prepared to wait indefinitely and both for the same unexplained reason: they had faith in Hamilton's powers of survival. And so Kellner had his hovercraft lit up like a Christmas tree. He was taking no chances that the helicopter would bypass him in the darkness.

He and Hiller, both men with their machine-pistols immediately and constantly ready to hand, stood on the brief afterdeck between the fans, ears always straining for the first faint intimation of the rackety clamour of the Sikorsky. But it was his eyes that gave Kellner the answer he was waiting for, not his ears. He peered upriver, peered more closely, then switched on and trained the hovercraft's powerful searchlight.

A powerless but impassively manned motor-launch and two canoes had just appeared in line ahead round a bend in the Rio da Morte.

7

The hovercraft's cabin was luxuriously furnished although on a necessarily small scale. The bar was splendidly if selectively equipped and, at the moment, well patronised. Most of the passengers from the wrecked helicopter gave the impression of having escaped from the jaws of death. The atmosphere was relaxed, almost convivial, and the spirit of the departed Heffner did not appear to hover over the company.

Hamilton said to Kellner: 'Any trouble during the night?'

'Not really. A couple of canoe-loads of Indians approached us just after midnight. We turned the searchlight on them and they turned and headed back for shore.'

'No shooting?'

'None.'

'Good. Now, the big question tomorrow is the rapids that the Indians call the Hoehna.'

'Rapids?' Kellner said. 'There are no rapids shown on the chart.'

'I daresay. Nevertheless, they're there. Never been through them myself although I've seen them from the air. Don't look anything special from up there, but then nothing ever does. Much experience with rapids?'

'A fair bit,' Kellner said. 'Nothing that a boat hasn't navigated though.'

'I'm told boats have made it through the Hoehna.'

'So where's the problem? A hovercraft can navigate rapids that no boat made by man could ever hope to.'

Serrano said: 'Knowing you, Señor Hamilton, I thought you would have had us on our way by this time. A clear night. Bright moon. A beautiful night for sailing. Or is it 'flying' in one of those machines?'

'We need a good night's rest, all of us. It's going to be a hard day tomorrow. The Hoehna rapids are less than a hundred miles away. How long to get there, Kellner?'

'Three hours. Less, if you want.'

'One does not navigate rapids by night. And only a madman goes there in the hours of darkness. Because of the Horena, you see.'

Tracy said: 'The Horena? Another Indian tribe?'

'Yes.'

'Like the Chapate?'

'They're not at all like the Chapate. The Horena are the Roman lions, the Chapate the Christians. The Horena put the fear of living

161

death into the Chapate.'

'But you said the Muscias — '

'Ah! The Muscias are to the Horena what the Horena are to the Chapate. Or so they say. Goodnight!'

★　★　★

'Rapids!' Ramon called out. 'Rapids ahead!'

In the two and a half hours since the hovercraft's dawn departure the Rio da Morte, though flowing at a rate of about fifteen knots, had been almost glassily calm and, although visibility had been poor because of fairly heavy rain, no problems had been encountered. But now conditions had dramatically altered. At first indistinctly through the now sheeting rain, but then suddenly, frighteningly, and all too vividly rocks could be seen, some jagged, some curved, thrusting up from the river bed. For as far as the eye could see hundreds of them spanned the entire width of the river with white-veined, seething water coursing down between them. The hovercraft, throttled back to a point where directional control could just be maintained, was almost at once into this white and seething cauldron.

When Kellner had said that he had some little experience of navigating rapids he had been doing himself less than justice. As far as the untrained observer could see, he was masterly. He was positively dancing a jig at the controls. He no longer had the throttle pulled back but kept altering it between half and full ahead which, considering their speed, might have seemed foolhardy, but wasn't. By doing this and by ignoring the air ducts and maintaining the cushion pressure as high as possible he could all the more easily avoid making violent course alterations which would have slewed the hovercraft broadside and into disaster. Instead, he was deliberately aiming for and riding his hovercraft over the less fearsome rocks in his path. Even here he had to be selective, searching out the more rounded rocks and avoiding the jagged ones which, at that speed, would have ripped even the abnormally tough apron skirts, leading to the collapse of the cushion and turning the hovercraft into a boat which would then have foundered in short order. One moment he was jerking the pitch control back, putting power on the left fan, then if this proved insufficient, applying right rudder to give him directional stability while only seconds later he had to reverse the procedure. His task was made harder by the fact that even the high-speed windscreen wipers were capable only intermittently of clearing the spray and rain.

Kellner said to Hamilton who was seated beside him: 'Tell me again about all those boats that were supposed to navigate the Hoehna.'

'I guess I must have been misinformed.'

Further back in the hovercraft no-one spoke because all their energies were concentrated on hanging on to their seats. The general effect of the motion was that of a roller-coaster — except that this roller-coaster, unlike the fairground type, also shook violently from side to side.

Up front, Kellner said: 'Do you see what I see?'

Some fifty yards ahead the river appeared to come to an abrupt end. They were obviously approaching a waterfall of sorts.

'Unfortunately. What are you going to do about it?'

'Funny.'

The hovercraft was being swept helplessly along to what was indeed a waterfall. The drop in the river level must have been at least ten feet. Kellner was doing the only thing he could do — trying to keep the hovercraft on a perfectly straight course.

The hovercraft swept over the fall, dipped

sharply and plunged downwards at an angle of forty-five degrees. With an explosion of sound and spray, the hovercraft momentarily disappeared save for the stern. Not only the bows but part of the front of the cabin had gone completely under and in that way and at that angle the hovercraft remained for several seconds before it slowly struggled to the surface again, water cascading off its decks. It settled deeper in the water, the effect of partially losing its air cushion when the stern had come completely clear of the water.

The interior of the craft was a scene of appalling confusion. The angle of fall and the stunning impact had catapulted everyone to the deck. Equipment which had been stored but not lashed aft was now scattered throughout the cabin. To make matters worse, a window had been smashed and hundreds of gallons of water were sloshing about the interior of the cabin. One by one the passengers struggled upright. They were bruised, dazed and slightly concussed, but there seemed to be no broken bones.

As the air cushion began to fill again and the water gurgled away through the self-draining ports, they could feel the hovercraft rise slowly to its normal position.

Three times in the next few minutes the hovercraft went through a similar experience, although none of the waterfalls were as high as the first time. At last the hovercraft passed into an area of smooth, rock-free water, but it was then that another danger manifested itself. The forested banks gave way to what was at first low rock, which quickly became higher and higher until they were passing through what was virtually a cliff-sided canyon. At the same time the river swiftly narrowed to about a third of its original width and the speed of the river and hence that of the hovercraft rapidly more than doubled.

Hamilton and Kellner stared through the windscreens, glanced at each other, then looked forward again. Ahead, the steep-sided river walls fell sharply away, but this promised no surcease. A quarter of a mile ahead a jumble of huge black rocks blocked the river from side to side.

'Bloody charts!' Kellner said.

'Indeed.'

'Pity, really. These machines are very expensive.'

'Make for the left.'

'Any particular reason?'

'The Horena live on the right bank.'

'Left, as the man says.'

The rocks were about three hundred yards away. They appeared to form an impenetrable barrier, no two sufficiently far apart to afford passage to the hovercraft.

Hamilton and Kellner looked at each other. Simultaneously they shrugged. Hamilton turned and faced the rear.

'Hang on tight,' he said. 'We're about to stop very suddenly.' He had no sooner spoken than he realised that his warning had been unnecessary. They had seen what was coming up. They were already hanging on for dear life.

The rocks were now no more than a hundred yards distant. Kellner was guiding the craft towards the biggest gap between any two of them, the first and the second from the left bank.

For one brief moment it seemed that the hovercraft might just have one chance of making the passage as Kellner arrowed straight for the centre of the gap. The craft's bows passed through but that was all: the passage was at least eighteen inches narrower than the midships beam of the hovercraft. With a grinding, screeching tearing of metal, the hovercraft came to an abrupt halt, immovably jammed.

Kellner went into reverse and applied maximum power. Nothing happened. Kellner eased off the fans but kept the engine running to maintain the cushion. He straightened up, muttering to himself, 'Now with an ocean-going tug ... '

* * *

Ten minutes later there was a pile of rucksacks, canvas bags and other improvised luggage containers on deck and Hamilton was securing a rope around his waist. He said: 'It's only twenty feet to that bank but the water's mighty fast so kindly don't let go of the end of that rope.'

It was a danger, but not the only one. Even as he finished speaking there came a sudden grunt and Kellner collapsed to the deck. A dart protruded from the back of his neck. Hamilton swung round.

On the far right bank, less than fifty yards away, stood a group of Indians, ten or twelve in all. Every man had a blowpipe to his mouth.

'Horena!' Hamilton shouted. 'Down! Take cover behind the cabin, inside the cabin. Ramon! Navarro!'

Almost immediately, Ramon and Navarro, all humanitarian principles forgotten at the sight of Kellner, were on the cabin roof, stretched out on their elbows, rifles in hand. More darts struck the metal sheathing but none found a target. In three seconds the twins fired six shots. At five hundred yards either man was accurate. At fifty yards they were deadly. One after another, in those few seconds, three Horena toppled into the river, three others crumpled and died where they stood, and the others melted away.

Hamilton gazed down in bitterness at the lifeless Kellner. Not for the Horena the use of timbo, the poisonous bark of a forest vine which merely stunned: the dart which took Kellner had been tipped with curare.

Hamilton said: 'If it weren't for Kellner we'd all be dead. And now Kellner is dead.' Without another word he jumped into the river. The only danger here was the speed of the water: neither alligators nor piranha ever inhabit rapids.

At first he was swept downstream and had to be hauled back. On the second attempt he succeeded in reaching the bank. He stood there some time, regaining his breath — the buffeting had been severe — then undid the rope around his waist and secured it to the bole of a tree. Another rope was thrown across to him. This he passed round a branch and threw back to the hovercraft where, in turn, it was passed round a fan bracket and thrown back to Hamilton, forming, in effect, an endless pulley.

The first item of equipment — Hamilton's

own rucksack — was ferried across, well clear of the water, as was all the rest of the equipment. The members of the party had to make it the wet way.

8

Sweat-soaked and stumbling, mostly from near exhaustion, the heavily laden party of nine made their painfully slow way through the afternoon gloom of the rainforest. Even at high noon there was never more than half-light in its depths. The crowns of the great liana-festooned trees stretched out and intertwined a hundred feet or more above the ground, effectively blocking out the sunlight.

Progress was not slow because they had to hack their way with machetes through the dense undergrowth, because of dense undergrowth there was none. For plants to grow at ground-level, sunshine is essential. Jungle, in the true African sense of the term, did not exist. The progress was slow primarily because there was as much swampland as there was firm ground and quicksands were an ever-present peril. A man could step confidently on to what appeared to be an inviting stretch of greensward and on his second step find himself shoulder deep in a swamp. For safe locomotion in the forest, a probe, in the form of a hacked-off and trimmed branch, was essential. For every mile covered as the crow flew, it was not uncommon to have to traverse five miles. That, and the time it took to locate patches of firm ground, made for time-consuming, frustrating and exhausting travel.

Smith, in particular, was making heavy weather of it. His clothes were so saturated with sweat that he might well have just been dragged from the river. His legs had gone rubbery and he was gasping for breath.

Smith said: 'What the hell are you trying to prove, Hamilton? How tough you are and how out of condition we city dwellers are? God's sake, man, a break. An hour wouldn't kill us, would it?'

'No. But the Horena might.'

'But you said their territory was on the right bank.'

'That's what I believe. But don't forget: we killed six of their men. Great lads for revenge, the Horena. I wouldn't put it past them to have crossed the river and be following us. There could be a hundred of them within a hundred yards of here, just waiting to get within blowpipe range, and we wouldn't know a thing about it until too late.'

Smith, it appeared, was possessed of reserves of strength and endurance of which he had been unaware. He hurried on.

Towards evening, they reached a small and largely swampy clearing. Most of the party were now shambling, not walking.

'Enough,' Hamilton said. 'We'll make camp.'

With the approach of dusk the forest appeared to come alive. All around them was sound. Mainly, it came from birds — parrots, macaws, parakeets. But there was animal life too. Monkeys screeched, bull-frogs barked and now and again the deeply muffled roar of a jaguar came at them from the depths of the forest.

Everywhere there were creepers, vines, parasitic orchids and there, in the clearing, exotic flowers of almost every conceivable colour. The air was damp and fetid, a miasmic smell all-prevalent, the heat over-powering and leaden and enervating, the floor underfoot almost an unbroken expanse of thick, clinging, evil-smelling mud.

Everyone, even Hamilton, sank gratefully to what few patches of dry ground they could find. Over the river, not much higher than the tree-tops, several birds, with huge wing-spreads, seemed suspended against the sky, for their wings were motionless. They looked evil, sinister.

Maria said: 'What are those horrible-looking creatures?'

'Urubus,' Hamilton said. 'Amazonian vultures. They seem to be looking for something.'

Maria shuddered. Everybody gazed unhappily at the vultures.

'A poor choice, I suppose,' Hamilton said. 'The cooking-pots, head-hunters or the vultures. And speaking of cooking-pots, some fresh meat might help. Curassow — a kind of wild turkey — armadillo, wild boar, all very tasty. Navarro?'

Ramon said: 'I'll come too.'

'You stay, Ramon. A little more thoughtfulness, please. Someone has to look after these poor souls.'

Tracy said: 'To keep an eye on us, you mean.'

'I don't see what mischief you can get up to here.'

'Your haversack.'

'I don't understand.'

Tracy said deliberately: 'Heffner appeared to find something there just before you murdered him.'

Ramon said: 'Before Mr Heffner met his unfortunate end is what Mr Tracy means.'

Hamilton eyed Tracy thoughtfully then turned away into the forest, Navarro following. Less than two hundred yards from the camp Hamilton put a restraining hand on

Navarro's arm and pointed ahead. Not forty yards away was a *quiexada,* that most savage of all the world's wild boars. They are so devoid of fear that they have been known to invade towns in herds, driving the citizens into their houses.

'Supper,' Hamilton said.

Navarro nodded and raised his rifle. One single shot was all that Navarro would ever need. They began to make their way towards the dead animal then halted abruptly. A herd of perhaps three dozen *quiexada* had suddenly appeared from the forest. They halted, pawed the ground, then came on again. There was no mistaking their intention.

Only on the riversides do Amazonian trees have branches, for only there can they get sunlight. Hamilton and Navarro reached the lowermost branches of the nearest tree a short distance ahead of the boars, which proceeded to encircle the tree and then, as if in response to some unseen signal, began to use their vicious tusks to savage the roots of the tree. The roots of the Amazonian trees, like those of the giant sequoia of California, are extremely long — and extremely shallow.

'I would say they have done this sort of thing before,' Navarro said. 'How long is this going to take, do you think?'

'Not long at all.'

Hamilton sighted his pistol and shot a *quiexada* that seemed to be more industrious than its companions. The dead animal toppled into the river. Within seconds, the smooth surface of the river was disturbed by a myriad ripples and there came the high-pitched, spine-chilling buzzing whine as the needle teeth of the voracious piranha proceeded to strip the *quiexada* to the bone.

Navarro cleared his throat and said: 'Perhaps you should have shot one not quite so close to the river.'

Hamilton said: '*Quiexada* to one side, piranha to the other. You don't by any chance see a constrictor lurking in the branches above?'

Involuntarily, Navarro glanced upwards, then down at the boars which had redoubled their efforts. Both men started firing and within seconds a dozen *quiexada* lay dead.

Navarro said: 'Next time I go boar-hunting — if there is a next time — I shall bring a sub-machinegun with me. My magazine is empty.'

'Mine too.'

The sight of their dead companions seemed only to increase the blood lust of the boars. They tore at the roots with savage frenzy — and, already, several of the roots had been severed.

Navarro said: 'Señor Hamilton, either I'm

shaking or this tree is becoming rather
— what is the word for it?'

'Wobbly?'

'Wobbly.'

'I don't think. I know.'

A rifle shot rang out and a boar dropped
dead. Hamilton and Navarro swung round to
look back the way they had come. Ramon,
who seemed to be carrying a pack of some
sort on his back, was less than forty yards
away and was prudently standing by a
low-branched tree. He fired steadily and with
deadly accuracy. Suddenly an empty click was
heard. Hamilton and Navarro looked at each
other thoughtfully, but Ramon remained
unperturbed. He reached into his pocket,
extracted another magazine clip, fitted it and
resumed firing. Three more shots and it
finally dawned on the *quiexada* that they were
on to a hiding to nothing. Those that
remained turned and ran off into the forest.

The three men walked back towards the
camp, dragging a *quiexada* behind them.
Ramon said: 'I heard the shooting so I came.
Of course, I brought plenty of spare
ammunition with me.' Deadpan, he patted a
bulging pocket, then shrugged apologetically.
'All my fault. I should never have let you go
alone. One has to be a man of the forest — '

'Oh, shut up,' Hamilton said. 'Thoughtful

of you to bring my rucksack along with you.'

Ramon said pontifically: 'One should not expose the weak-minded to temptation.'

'Do be quiet,' Navarro said. He turned to Hamilton. 'God only knows he was insufferable enough before. But now, after this — '

*　*　*

The cooking fire burned in the near darkness and boar steaks sizzled in a glowing bed of coals.

Smith said: 'I appreciate the necessity for all the shots. But if the Horena are around — well, that must have attracted the attention of everyone within miles.'

'No worry,' Hamilton said. 'No Horena will ever attack at night. If he dies at night his soul will wander for ever in the hereafter. His gods must see him die.' He prodded a steak with his sheath knife. 'I would say those are just about ready.' Ready or not, the steaks were dispatched with every sign of gusto and when they were finished Hamilton said: 'Better if it had hung a week, but tasty, tasty. Bed. We leave at dawn. I'll keep the first watch.'

They prepared for sleep, some lying on waterproof sheets, others in lightweight hammocks slung between trees at the edge of the clearing. Hamilton flung some fuel on the

178

fire and kept on flinging it until it flared up so brightly that the flames were almost ten feet high. Machete in hand, Hamilton departed to obtain some more fuel and returned with an armful of branches most of which he cast on the already blazing fire.

Smith said: 'Well, granted, granted, you know how to make bonfires. But what's it all in aid of?'

'Safety measures. Keeps the creepy-crawlies at bay. Wild animals fear fire.' He was to be proved half right, half wrong.

He was on his third fuel-hunting trip and was returning to camp when he heard the piercing scream of fear. He dropped the fuel and ran into the brightly lit clearing. He knew the high-pitched scream could only have come from Maria and as he closed on her hammock the reason for her terror was obvious: a giant anaconda, at least thirty feet in length and with its tail still anchored to one of the trees that supported Maria's hammock, had one of its deadly coils wrapped round the base of her hammock. She was in no way pinned down, just too paralysed with fear to move. The anaconda's vast jaws were agape.

It was not Hamilton's first anaconda and he had a nodding respect for them but no more. A full-grown specimen can swallow a

150-pound deer in its entirety. But while they could be endlessly patient, even cunning, in waiting for their next meal to come along, they were extremely slow-witted in action. While Maria continued to scream in the same mindless terror, he approached within feet of the fearsome head. No more than any other creature on earth could an anaconda withstand three Luger bullets in the head: it died immediately, but even in its death the coil slipped over the girl's ankles and continued to contract. Hamilton struggled to pull the leathery coil free but was brushed aside by Ramon who carefully placed two rifle bullets into the upper centre of the coil, severing the main spinal nerve. The anaconda at once went limp.

Hamilton carried her across to his ground-sheet close by the fire. She was in a state of mild shock. Keep a shocked patient warm, Hamilton had often heard, and the thought had no sooner occurred to him than Ramon knelt alongside, a sleeping-bag in his hands. Together they eased the girl inside, zipped up the bag and sat to wait. Navarro came to join them and jerked a thumb in the direction of an apparently sleeping Smith.

'Observe our gallant hero,' he said. 'Asleep? He's wide awake. Has been all the time. I watched him.'

Ramon said complainingly: 'You might have come and watched us.'

'When you and Señor Hamilton can't take care of a simple-minded reptile like that it's time for us all to retire. I saw his face and he was terrified, seemed quite unable to move: not, I am sure, that he wanted to move or had any intention of moving. Has the girl been hurt?'

'Not physically,' Hamilton said. 'I'm afraid this is basically my fault. I had a big fire going to frighten off wild animals. Well, anacondas are also wild creatures and as frightened of fire as any other. This one just wanted out: it was the devil's bad luck that it was roosting in the tree that helped support Maria's hammock. I'm pretty sure she would have come to no harm. The reptile was simply easing its way down the tree. Apart from the fact that its belly is swollen and obviously would not be requiring another meal for a fortnight, it probably had a much greater matter on its mind, such as getting the hell out of here. All very unfortunate but no harm done.'

'Perhaps,' Ramon said. 'I hope.'

'You hope?' Hamilton said.

'Trauma,' Ramon said. 'How deep does a trauma lie? This has been a traumatic experience. But I think that's only a side issue. I have the feeling that her whole life has

181

been a traumatic experience.'

'You plunging into the deep waters of psychology, psychiatry or what-have-you, Ramon?' Hamilton didn't smile as he spoke.

'I agree with Ramon,' Navarro said. 'Twins, you know,' he added apologetically. 'Something is wrong or not what it appears to be. Her actions, her behaviour, the way she talks and smiles — I find it hard to believe that this is a bad person, a common whore. Smith, we know, *is* a bad person. She doesn't care for him, any fool can see that. So what goes on?'

'Well,' Hamilton said judicially, 'he's got a lot to offer — '

'Ignore Señor Hamilton,' Ramon said. 'He's just trying to provoke us.'

Navarro nodded in agreement then said: 'I think she is a prisoner in some way or another.'

'Possibly,' Hamilton said. 'Possibly. Has it occurred to either of you that *he* might be in some way *her* prisoner, without ever knowing it?'

Navarro looked at Ramon, then accusingly at Hamilton. 'There you go again, Señor Hamilton. You know something that we don't know and you're not telling us.'

'I know nothing that you don't know and far be it from me to suggest that I look more closely and, perhaps, think a little more

182

deeply. But, then, you are young.'

'Young?' Navarro was indignant. 'Neither of us, Señor Hamilton, will ever see thirty again.'

'That's what I meant.' He put his fingers to his lips. Beside him, Maria was stirring. She opened her eyes, still huge with fear and horror. Hamilton touched her gently on the shoulder.

'It's all right now,' he said gently. 'It's all over.'

'That horrible, ghastly head.' Her voice was no more than a husky whisper and she was shaking. Ramon rose and walked away. 'That awful snake — '

'The snake is dead,' Hamilton said. 'And you are unharmed. We promise you, no harm will come to you.'

She lay there breathing shallowly, her eyes closed. She opened them again when Ramon returned and knelt by her side. He had an aluminium cup in one hand, a bottle in the other.

Hamilton said: 'And what do we have here?'

'The finest cognac,' Ramon replied. 'As is only to be expected. Smith's private supplies.'

'I don't like brandy,' she said.

'Ramon is right. You'd better like it. You need it.'

Ramon poured a generous measure. She tasted it, coughed, screwed her eyes shut and emptied the cup in two gulps.

'Good girl,' Hamilton said.

'Awful,' she said. She looked at Ramon. 'But thank you. I feel better already.' She glanced across the clearing and fear touched her eyes again. 'That hammock — '

'You're not going back to that hammock,' Hamilton said. 'It's safe enough now, of course, it was just sheer bad luck that the anaconda was up the tree when your hammock was slung, but we can understand your not wanting to go back there. You're in Ramon's sleeping-bag and on a ground-sheet. You'll stay just where you are. We'll keep a big fire going all night and one of the three of us will keep an eye on you till the morning. Come the dawn, I promise you not even a mosquito will have come near you.'

Slowly she looked at the three men in turn then said huskily: 'You are all very kind to me.' She tried to smile but it was only a try. 'Damsel in distress. Is that it?'

'Perhaps there's a little bit more to it than that,' Hamilton said. 'But now's not the time to talk about it. Just you try to sleep — I'm sure Ramon will give you a night-cap to help you on your way. Oh, hell.'

Smith, who obviously felt that he had

maintained his distance long enough, was approaching, his whole attitude manifesting his resentment of Maria's close proximity to the three men. As he dropped to his knees beside her, Hamilton rose, looked at him, turned and walked away, the twins following.

Ramon said: 'Señor Hamilton. *Quiexada*, piranha, anaconda, a sick girl and a villain. To pick so divine a resting spot in such unique company is a gift not given to many.'

Hamilton just looked at him and moved off into the forest to retrieve his load of firewood.

* * *

Early in the morning Hamilton led the others in single file through the rainforest and across firm ground, firm because the terrain was gently rising and the water table was now well below them. After about two hours' walking Hamilton stopped and waited until the others gathered round him.

'From here on,' Hamilton said, 'no talking. Not one word. And watch where you put your feet. I don't want to hear as much as the crackle of a broken twig. Understood?' He looked at Maria, who looked pale and exhausted, not so much from the rigours of the walk, for there had been none, but

185

because she had not slept at all: the previous night's experience, as Ramon had said, had been something more than traumatic. 'It's not much further. Half an hour, at most, then we'll have a rest and carry on during the afternoon.'

'I'm all right,' she said. 'It's just that I'm beginning to hate this rainforest. I suppose you'll be telling me again that no-one asked me to come.'

'A snake on every tree, is that it?' She nodded. 'No more worry,' Hamilton said. 'You'll never again spend a night in the forest. That's another promise.'

Tracy said slowly: 'I take it that that can mean only one thing. I take it that we'll be in the Lost City tonight.'

'If things go as I hope, yes.'

'You know where you are?'

'Yes.'

'You've known ever since we left the hovercraft.'

'True. How did you know?'

'Because you haven't used your compass since.'

* * *

Half an hour later, exactly as he had forecast, Hamilton, finger to his lips, stopped and

186

waited for the others to come up to him. When he spoke, it was in a whisper.

'On your lives. Not a sound. Stay hidden until I tell you otherwise. On your hands and knees then lie prone until I give the word.'

And so on hands and knees they advanced in total silence. Hamilton dropped forward and eased himself slowly ahead, using elbows and toes. He stopped again and waited until the others had joined him. He pointed forward, through the trees. In a lush green valley below them they could see an Indian village. There were dozens of large huts and, in the centre, a very large communal hut, which looked as if it could accommodate at least two hundred people with ease. The place seemed to be deserted until suddenly a small copper-coloured child appeared carrying a flint axe and a nut which he placed on a flat stone and proceeded to belabour. It was like a scene from the Stone Age, from the dawn of prehistory. A laughing woman, statuesque and also copper-coloured, emerged from the same hut and picked up the child.

In slow wonderment, Tracy said: 'That colour? That appearance? Those aren't Indians.'

'Keep your voice down,' Hamilton said urgently. 'They're Indians all right but they do not come from the Amazon basin. They

187

come from the Pacific.'

Tracy stared at him, still in wonderment, and shook his head.

Suddenly people, scores of them, began to emerge from the communal hut. That they were not Amazonian Indians was obvious from the fact that there were as many women as men among them: normally, in the Amazonian basin, women are banned from the meeting places of elders and warriors. All were of the same copper colour, all possessed of a proud, almost regal bearing. They began to disperse towards their huts.

Smith touched Hamilton on the arm and said in a low voice: 'Who are those people?'

'The Muscias.' Smith turned pale.

'Goddamned Muscias!' he said in a vicious whisper. 'What the hell are you playing at? Head-hunters, you said. Head-shrinkers! Cannibals! I'm off!'

'Off where, you clown? You've got no place left to run to. Stay here. *Don't, don't, don't* show yourselves.'

The advice was probably superfluous. No-one, clearly, had the slightest intention of showing himself.

Hamilton rose and walked confidently into the clearing. He had gone at least ten paces before he was noticed. There was a sudden silence, the babble of voices ceased, then the chatter redoubled in volume. An exceptionally tall Indian, old and with his forearms almost covered in what were unquestionably gold bracelets, gazed for some seconds then ran forward. He and Hamilton embraced each other.

The old man, who was surely the chief, and Hamilton engaged in an animated, if incomprehensible, conversation. The chief, with an expression of incredulity on his face, repeatedly shook his head. Just as firmly Hamilton nodded his. Suddenly, Hamilton extended his right arm and made a semi-circular motion, bringing his arm to a sudden halt. The chief looked long at him, seized him by the arms, smiled and nodded his head. He turned and spoke rapidly to his people.

Tracy said: 'I'd say those two people have met somewhere before.'

The chief finished addressing his people, all of whom had now gathered in the clearing, and spoke again to Hamilton, who nodded and turned.

Hamilton shouted to his waiting companions: 'You can come now. Keep your hands well away from any weapon.'

Not quite dazedly, but not understanding what was happening, the other eight members of the party entered the clearing.

Hamilton said: 'This is Chief Corumba.' He introduced each of the eight in turn. The chief gravely acknowledged each introduction, shaking each in turn by hand.

Hiller said: 'But Indians don't shake hands.'

'This Indian does.'

Maria touched Hamilton on the arm. 'But those savage head-hunters — '

'These are the kindliest, most gentle, most peaceable people on earth. In their language they do not have a word for war because they do not know what war is. They are lost children from a lost age and the people who built the Lost City.'

Serrano said: 'And I thought I knew more about the tribes of the Mato Grosso than any man alive.'

'And so you may, Serrano, so you may. If, that is to say, I can take the word of Colonel Diaz.'

'Colonel Diaz?' Smith said. He was clearly floundering in deep water. 'Who's Colonel Diaz?'

'A friend of mine.'

Tracy said: 'But their ferocious reputation — '

'A fiction invented by Dr Hannibal Huston, the man who found these lost people. He thought that such a reputation might ensure them — what shall we say? — a little privacy.'

'Huston?' Hiller said. 'Huston? You — you found Huston?'

'Years ago.'

'But you've only been in the Mato Grosso for four months.'

'I have known it for many years. Remember in the Hotel de Paris in Romono you mentioned my search for the golden people? I forgot to mention that I also met them years ago. Here they are. The Children of the Sun.'

Maria said: 'And Dr Huston is still in the Lost City?'

'He's still there. Come, I believe these good people want to offer us some hospitality. First, however, I owe you a small explanation about them.'

'High time, too,' Smith said. 'Why all the dramatic, stealthy approach to them?'

'Because if we had approached as a group they would have run away. They have every good reason to fear those from the outside world. We, ironically known as the *civilizados* — in practically everything that matters they're a damned sight more civilised than we are — bring them so-called progress, which harms them, so-called change, which harms them, so-called civilisation, which harms them even more, and disease, which kills them. These people have no natural resistance to measles or influenza. Either of those are to them what bubonic plague was to Europeans and Asiatics in the Middle Ages. Half a tribe can be wiped out in a fortnight. The same thing happened to the people of Tierra del Fuego. Well-meaning missionaries gave them simple clothes, primarily so that the women could cover their nakedness. The blankets came from a hospital where there had been a measles epidemic. Most of the people were wiped out.'

Tracy said: 'But our presence here. Surely that endangers them?'

'No. Almost half the Muscias were destroyed by measles or influenza or a combination of both. These people here are the survivors, having acquired natural immunity the hard way. As I said, it was Dr Huston who found them. Although mainly famous as an explorer, his real life's work lay elsewhere. He was one of the original *sertanistas* — men wise in jungle ways — and a founder member of the FUNAI, the National Foundation for the Indian, people who dedicate their lives to protecting the Indians and rendering them harmless to *civilizados*. 'Pacification' is the term generally used but in truth what they mainly required was protection *against* the *civilizados*. Sure, many of the tribes were genuinely savage — well, not so many, there are less than two hundred thousand pure-blood Indians left — but their savagery sprang from fear and very understandably so. Even in modern times, those civilised gentlemen from the outer world, and by no means all Brazilians, either, have machine-gunned them, dynamited them from the air and given them poisoned food.'

'This is all news to me,' Smith said, 'and I've lived in this country for many years. Frankly, I find it very hard to believe.'

'Serrano will confirm it.'

'I confirm it. I take it that you, too, are a *sertanista*.'

'Yes. Not always a very happy job. We have our failures. The Chapate and the Horena, as you've seen, are not too keen on the idea of co-operation with the outside world. And, inevitably, we bring disease as we did here. Come along, Chief Corumba is summoning us to eat. It may taste a little odd, but I can assure you that no harm will come to any of you.'

★ ★ ★

One hour later the visitors were still seated around a rough wooden table outside the communal hut. Before them lay the remains of an excellent if rather exotic meal — game, fish, fruit and other unknown delicacies concerning the nature of which it had been thought more prudent not to ask: all had been washed down with *cachassa*, a rather potent brew. At the end, Hamilton thanked Chief Corumba on behalf of all of them and turned to the others.

'I think it's time we were on our way.'

Tracy said: 'One thing intrigues me. I've never seen so many gold ornaments in my life.'

'I thought that might intrigue you.'

'Where do these people come from?'

'They don't know themselves. A lost people who have lost everything and that includes their history. It was Dr Huston's theory that they are the descendants of the Quimbaya, an ancient tribe from the Cauca or Magdalena valleys in the western Andes of Colombia.'

Smith stared at him. 'So what in God's name are they doing here?'

'Nobody knows. Huston thinks they left their homeland all those hundreds of years ago. He thinks they may have fled to the east, found the headwaters of the Amazon, come

194

all the way down until they reached the Rio Tocantis, turned up that until they came to the Araguaia, then up the Rio da Morte. Again, who knows? Stranger migrations have happened. It could have taken them generations: they were weighed down with many possessions. I believe it. Wait till you see the Lost City and you'll understand why I do believe it.'

Smith said: 'How far away is this damned city?'

'Five hours. Six.'

'Five hours!'

'And easy going. Uphill, but no swamps, no quicksands.' He turned to Chief Corumba, who smiled and again warmly embraced Hamilton.

'Wishing us good luck?' Smith said.

'Among quite a few other things. I'll have a longer chat with him tomorrow.'

'Tomorrow!'

'Why ever not?'

Smith, Tracy and Hiller exchanged flickering glances. None of the three said anything.

Just before they walked away Hamilton spoke quietly to Maria. 'Stay behind with these people. They will look after you, I promise. Where we're going is no place for a lady.'

'I'm coming.'

'Suit yourself. There's an excellent chance you'll be dead by nightfall.'

'You don't much care for me, do you?'

'Enough to ask you to stay behind.'

* * *

In the late afternoon Hamilton and his party were still making their way towards the Lost City. The going underfoot was excellent, dry, leafy and springy.

Unfortunately for people like Smith, the incline was fairly severe and the heat was, of course, as always oppressive.

Hamilton said: 'I think we'll have a half-hour break here. We're ahead of time — we can't move in until it's dark. Besides, some of you may think you've earned a rest.'

'Too bloody right, we have,' Smith said. 'How much longer do you intend to crucify us?'

He sank wearily to the ground and mopped his streaming face with a bandana. He was not the only one to do so. With the exception of Hamilton and the twins, everyone seemed to be suffering from a shortage of breath and leaden, aching legs. Hamilton had, indeed, been setting a brisk pace.

'You've done very well, all of you,' Hamilton said. 'Mind you, you might have done even better if you hadn't guzzled and drunk like pigs down in the village. We've climbed almost two thousand feet since leaving there.'

Smith said: 'How — much — longer?'

'From here to the top? Another half hour. No more. I'm afraid we'll have to do a bit more climbing after that — downhill, mind you, but a pretty steep downhill.'

'Half an hour,' Smith said. 'Nothing.'

'Wait until you start going down.'

★ ★ ★

'The last lap,' Hamilton said. 'We are ten yards from the brink of a ravine. Anyone who hasn't a head for heights had better say so now.'

If anyone didn't have a head for heights he or she wasn't saying so. Hamilton began to crawl forward. The rest followed. Hamilton stopped and motioned to the others to join him.

Hamilton said: 'You see what I see?'

Smith said: 'Jesus!'

Maria said: 'The Lost City!'

Tracy said: 'Shangri-la!'

'El Dorado,' Hamilton said.

'What?' Smith said. 'What was that?'

'Nothing, really. There never was an El

Dorado. It means the golden man. New Inca rulers were covered in gold dust and dipped — only temporarily, of course — in a lake. You see that peculiar stepped pyramid with the flat top at the far end?'

The question was really unnecessary. It was the dominant feature of the Lost City.

'That's one of the reasons — there are two others — why Huston thought that the Children of the Sun came from Colombia. It's what you call a ziggurat. Originally it was a temple tower in Babylonia or Assyria. No traces of those remain in the Old World — the Egyptians built a quite different form of pyramid.'

Tracy said, as if not knowing: 'This is the only one?'

'By no means. You'll find well-preserved examples in Mexico, Guatemala, Bolivia and Peru. But only in Central America and the north-west of South America. But nowhere else in the world — except here.'

Serrano said: 'So they're Andean. You couldn't ask for better proof.'

'You couldn't. But I have it.'

'Complete proof? Total?'

'I'll show you later.' He pointed with outstretched arm. 'You see those steps?'

Stretching from the river to the top of the plateau and hewn from the vertical rock-face, the stone stairway, terrifying to look at even from a distance, angled upwards at 45°.

'Two hundred and forty-eight steps,' Hamilton said, 'each thirty inches wide. Worn, smooth and slippery — and no hand rail.'

Tracy said: 'Who counted them?'

'I did.'

'You mean — '

'Yes. Wouldn't do it again, though. There had been a hand rail once and I'd brought along equipment to rig a rope rail. It's still on the hovercraft — for obvious reasons.'

'Mr Hamilton!' Silver spoke in an urgent whisper. 'Mr Hamilton!'

'What's the excitement about?'

'I saw someone moving in the ruins down there. I swear to it.'

'The pilot's eagle-eye, eh? No need to swear to anything. There are quite a number of people down there. Why do you think I didn't fly in by helicopter?'

Serrano said: 'They are not friends, no?'

'No.' He turned to Smith. 'Speaking of helicopters, I don't have to explain the layout of this place to you. You know it already.'

'I don't understand.'

'That film cassette you had Hiller steal for you.'

'I don't know what — '

'I took them a year ago. I left Hiller no option but to steal them. Taken from a helicopter. Not bad for an amateur, were they?'

Smith didn't say whether they were or not. He, Hiller and Tracy had again, momentarily, assumed very odd expressions, mainly of deep unease.

Hamilton said: 'Look to your left there. Just where the river forks to go round the island.'

At a distance of about half a mile and about three hundred feet below their present elevation a spidery, sagging, and apparently twisted series of ropes spanned the gorge between the top of the plateau and a point about half-way up the top of the cliff on which they were lying. Immediately below the cliff anchorage a small waterfall arced out into the river.

'A rope bridge,' Hamilton said. 'Well, a liana bridge. Or a straw bridge. Those are normally renewed once a year. This one can't have been renewed for at least five years. Must be in a pretty rotten state by this time.'

'So?' Smith said. The apprehension in his voice was unmistakable.

'So that's the way we go in.'

The silence that followed was long and profound.

At last Serrano said 'Another proof of Andean ancestry, no? I mean, there *are* no rope bridges in the Mato Grosso — well, there's not one now — nor, as far as I know, anywhere in Brazil. The Indians never learnt how to make them. Why should they have done — they never needed them. But the Incas and their descendants knew how to make them — living in the Andes, they had to know.'

'I've seen one,' Hamilton said. 'On the Apurimac river, high up in Peru — about twelve thousand feet. They use six heavy braided straw cables for the main supports — four for the footpaths, two for the hand rails. Smaller ropes for closing in the sides and a bed of twigs spread over the footpath so that only a three-year-old could possibly fall through. Can support scores of people when new. I'm afraid this one is not new.'

A narrow cleft ran down the cliff at an angle of close on 60°. A small stream, probably fed from some spring above, fell, rather than flowed down this cleft, leaping whitely from spur to spur. On one side of this cleft a series of rough steps had been cut, obviously a very long time ago.

Hamilton and the others started to descend. It was a fairly arduous descent but not really either difficult or dangerous as

Hamilton had taken the precaution of binding together a series of tough lianas, anchoring one end to a tree and letting the rest fall down the cleft.

At the foot of the cleft, just above where the waterfall arced out above the river, a platform, about eight feet by eight, had been quarried out of the cliff-face. Hamilton was already standing there. One by one he was joined by the others.

Hamilton moved to examine a stone bollard and an iron post that had been hammered into the platform. Three now threadbare lianas were attached to both. Hamilton produced his sheath knife and scraped at the iron post. Thick brown flakes were shaved away.

'Keep your voices down,' Hamilton said. 'Rusty, isn't it?' He turned away to look over the gorge. The others did the same. The straw bridge was very flimsy and clearly venerable. Both the hand supports and the footpath were severely frayed. Several of the straw ropes appeared to have rotted and fallen away.

Hamilton said: 'Not in the best condition, wouldn't you say?'

Smith, his eyes wide, was obviously appalled. 'Good God in heaven. That's suicide. Only a madman would go on it. Do you expect me to risk my life on that?'

'Of course not. Why on earth should you? You're only here for the story, for the pictures. You'd be crazy to risk your life just for that. Tell you what. Give me your camera and I'll take the pictures for you. And don't forget — the people over there may not be welcoming to trespassers.'

Smith was silent for some time, then said: 'I'm a man who sees things through to the end.'

'Maybe the end is closer than you think. It's dark enough now. I'm going first.'

Navarro said: 'Señor Hamilton. I am much lighter — '

'Thank you. But that's just the point. I'm a heavy man and I'm carrying a heavy pack. If it takes my weight — well, you should all be okay.'

Ramon said: 'A thought occurs to me.'

'And to me.' He moved towards the straw bridge.

'What was that meant to mean?' Maria said.

'He thinks, perhaps, that they will have a welcome mat out over there.'

'Oh. A guard.'

Hamilton moved steadily across the straw bridge. That is, he made steady progress. The bridge itself was shockingly unsteady, swaying from side to side. Hamilton was now more than half-way across. The bridge sagged so badly in the middle that he had to haul himself up a fairly steep incline. But he was experiencing no great difficulty. He arrived safely on a platform similar to the one he had left on the other side of the gorge. He crouched low, for the platform was only a few feet lower than the plateau. Cautiously, he lifted his head.

There was, indeed, a guard, but he was not taking his duties too seriously. He was smoking a cigarette and, of all things, relaxing in a deck chair. Hamilton's bent arm was raised to shoulder level. His handkerchief-wrapped hand held the blade of his heavy sheath knife. The guard drew deeply on his cigarette, clearly illuminating his face. He made no sound as the haft of the knife struck him between the eyes, just tipped to one side and fell out of his chair.

Hamilton turned and flashed his torch three times. Within minutes he was joined one by one by eight people who had not enjoyed their passage across the rope bridge.

Hamilton said: 'Let's go and see the boss man.' He could find his way blindfolded and led them silently through the ancient ruins. Shortly he stopped and pointed.

There was a large and fairly new wooden

hall with lights showing. The sound of voices carried.

'Barracks,' Hamilton said. 'Mess hall and sleeping accommodation. Guards.'

Tracy said: 'Guards? Why?'

'Guilty conscience somewhere.'

'What's that noise?' Smith said.

'Generator.'

'Where do we go from here?'

'There.' Hamilton pointed again. At the foot of the giant ziggurat was another but much smaller wooden building. Lights also shone from that building.

'That's where the guilty conscience lives.' Hamilton was silent for a few moments. 'The man who every night feels dead feet trampling over his grave.'

Silver said: 'Mr Hamilton — '

'Nothing, nothing. Ramon, Navarro. I wonder if you see what I see?'

'Yes, indeed,' Ramon said. 'There are two men standing in the shadow of that porch.'

Hamilton seemed to ponder for a few moments. 'I wonder what they could be doing there?'

'We'll go and ask them.'

Ramon and Navarro melted into the shadows.

Smith said: 'Who are these two? Your assistants, I mean. They are not Brazilian.'

'No.'

'European?'

'Yes.'

Ramon and Navarro returned as silently and unobtrusively as they had left.

'Well,' Hamilton said. 'What did they say?'

'Not a great deal,' Navarro said. 'I think they may tell us when they wake up.'

9

Inside the smaller wooden house was a large
dining-cum-living-room. The walls were much
behung with flags, banners, portraits, swords,
rapiers, guns and pictures, all German. Behind
a table a large, rather red-faced, heavily jowled
man was eating a solitary meal to be washed
down by beer from a pewter litre mug beside
him. He looked up in amazement as the door
crashed open.

Hamilton, pistol in hand, entered. He was
followed by Smith, then the others.

'*Guten abend,*' Hamilton said. 'I've brought
an old friend along to see you.' He nodded
towards Smith. 'I think old friends should
smile and shake hands and say 'hallo', don't
you? You don't?'

Hamilton's pistol fired, gouging a hole in
the seated man's desk.

'Nervous hands,' Hamilton said. 'Ramon?'

Ramon went behind the desk and removed
a gun from an already half-opened drawer.

'Try the other drawer,' Hamilton said.
Ramon did so and came up with a second
gun.

'Can't really blame you,' Hamilton said.

'There are thieves and robbers everywhere these days. Well. Embarrassing silences bother me. Let me introduce you to each other. Behind the desk, Major-General Wolfgang Von Manteuffel of the S.S., variously known as Brown or Jones. Beside me, Colonel Heinrich Spaatz, also known as Smith, also of the S.S., Inspector General and Assistant Inspector General of the north and central Polish concentration and extermination camps, thieves on a colossal scale, murderers of old men in holy orders and despoilers of monasteries. Remember, that's where you last met — in that Grecian monastery where you cremated the monks. But, then, you were specialists in cremation, weren't you?'

They weren't saying whether they were or not. The stillness in the room was total. All eyes were on Hamilton with the exception of those of Von Manteuffel and Spaatz: they had eyes only for each other.

'Sad,' Hamilton said. 'Very sad. Spaatz came all this long way to see you, Von Manteuffel. Admittedly, he came to kill you, but he did come. Something, I believe, to do with a rainy night in the Wilhelmshaven docks.'

There came the sharp crack of a small-bore automatic. Hamilton looked at Tracy who, gun loose in an already nerveless hand, was sinking to the floor and from the state of his head it was clear he would never rise again. Maria had a gun in her hand and was very pale.

Hamilton said: 'My gun is on you.'

She put her automatic back in her bush jacket pocket. 'He was going to kill you.'

'He was,' Ramon said.

Hamilton looked at her in bafflement. '*He* was going to kill *me*, so *you* killed *him*?'

'I was waiting for it.'

Navarro said thoughtfully, 'I do believe the young lady is not all that we thought she was.'

'So it would seem.' Hamilton was equally thoughtful. He said to her: 'Whose side *are* you on?'

'Yours.'

Spaatz at last looked away from Von Manteuffel and stared at her in total incredulity. She went on quietly: 'It is sometimes quite difficult to tell a Jewish girl from other girls.'

Hamilton said: 'Israeli?'

'Yes.'

'Intelligence?'

'Yes.'

'Ah! Would you like to shoot Spaatz too?'

'They want him back in Tel Aviv.'

'Failing that?'

'Yes.'

'My apologies, and without any reservations. You're becoming quite unpopular, Spaatz. But not yet in Von Manteuffel's class. The Israelis want him for obvious reasons. The Greeks' — he nodded to Ramon and Navarro in turn — 'those two gentlemen are Greek army intelligence officers — want you for equally obvious reasons.' He looked at Hiller. 'They supplied me with those gold coins, by the way.' He turned back to Von Manteuffel. 'The Brazilian government want you for dispossessing the Muscia tribe and for the killing of many of them and *I* want you for the murder of Dr Hannibal Huston and his daughter, Lucy.'

Von Manteuffel smiled and spoke for the first time. 'I'm afraid you all want a great deal. And I'm afraid you're not going to get it.'

There came a loud crashing of glass and simultaneously the barrels of three sub-machine-guns protruded through three smashed windows.

Von Manteuffel smiled contentedly. 'Any person found with a gun on him will be shot out of hand. Do I have to tell you what to do next?'

He didn't. All guns were dropped on the floor, including two that Hamilton had not known that Spaatz and Hiller were carrying.

'So.' Von Manteuffel nodded in satisfaction.

'So much better than a blood bath, don't you think? Simpletons! How do you think I have survived for so long? By taking endless precautions. Such as this little press button my right foot rests on.'

He broke off as four armed men entered and watched them in silence as they searched the captives for further weapons. Predictably, they found none.

'And the rucksacks,' Von Manteuffel said.

Again the search failed to turn up any weapon.

Von Manteuffel said: 'I would have a word with my old friend Heinrich, who would appear to have come a very long way for nothing. Ah, and this man.' He indicated Hiller. 'I gather he's an accomplice of my dear ex-comrade in arms. The rest — take them and their pestilential luggage across to the old grain store. Perhaps I shall be subjecting them to some intensive and, I fear, very painful questioning. On the other hand, perhaps not. I shall decide after I've had my chat with Heinrich.'

10

The old grain store was built entirely of beautifully cut and fitted stone without any mortar whatsoever. It was about twenty feet by twelve, and had three storage bins on either side. The sides and the partitions of the bins were made of heavy adze-cut wood. A single weak and naked electric lamp, suspended from the ceiling, burned in the centre of the store. There were no windows and only one door-opening without a door, which the presence outside of a man with a cocked machine carbine made superfluous anyway. There were no furnishings of any description. Hamilton and his fellow captives had nothing to do but to look at each other or at the sentry, who faced them, his elderly but no doubt still lethal Schmeisser levelled directly at them: he had about him the look of a man who was yearning for an excuse to use it.

Navarro finally broke the silence. 'I fear for the health of our Mr Smith. Hiller, too, come to that.'

'Never mind about *their* damned health,' Hamilton said. 'Start fearing for your own.

When he's finished with those two who do you think is next on his list, whether or not he indulges in a little torture beforehand?' He sighed. 'Trust old trusty secret agent Hamilton to tell all. Von Manteuffel knows who I am, who Maria is, and who you two so-called Greek intelligence officers are. He can't let us live and I'm afraid he can't let Silver or Serrano live either — obviously.'

'In the meantime,' Serrano said, 'could I have a word with you?'

'Go ahead.'

'In private, if you please.'

'If that's what you want.' The two men moved to a corner of the room where Serrano spoke in a low rapid tone. Hamilton lifted his eyebrows and his face registered surprise, an emotion he had practically never betrayed. Then he shrugged his shoulders, nodded twice, turned thoughtfully away and looked at the sentry.

'Big man,' Hamilton said. 'My size. Black from head to toe — beret, jacket, trousers, shoes. I want those clothes. More importantly, I want that gun. Even more importantly still, I want them both fast.'

'Easy,' Ramon said. 'Just ask him.'

Hamilton didn't reply. Savagely, almost, and to the accompaniment of the indrawn hiss of Maria's breath, he bit the ball of his left thumb. At once the blood began to flow. He squeezed the torn flesh until the blood flowed even more freely, then smeared it over Ramon's uncomprehending face.

'All in the interest of art,' Hamilton told him. 'Brother, what a fight this is going to be.'

The 'fight' started in the corner of the store, just out of the sentry's line of sight. The sentry would have been less than human not to locate the source of the sound of the heavy blows, the shouting and swearing. He moved forward into the doorway.

Hamilton and Ramon were belabouring each other mightily, fighting in apparently vicious fury, kicking and punching and obviously intent on inflicting grievous and mutual bodily harm. The sentry was clearly startled, but not suspicious. He had a heavily brutalised face behind which there lurked no great intelligence.

'Stop that!' he shouted. 'You madmen! Stop it or — '

He broke off as one of the combatants received a seemingly murderous blow and came staggering to fall flat on his back, half in and half out of the doorway, eyes turned up in his head, the face masked with blood. The sentry stepped by him, ready to quell any further signs of trouble. Ramon's hands closed round his ankles.

Four men prepared to carry three blanket-covered, stretchered forms from Von Manteuffel's room. Von Manteuffel said: 'It can be fatal to allow an enemy to live longer than is necessary.' He paused, briefly, for thought. 'Over the side with them. Think of all those poor starving piranha. As for our other friends in the grain store, I don't think they can supply me with any more useful information. You know what to do.'

'Yes, Herr General,' one of the men said. 'We know what to do.' His face was wolfish in anticipation.

Von Manteuffel glanced at his watch. 'I will expect you back in exactly five minutes. After you've given the piranha their second course.'

★　★　★

A figure, dressed all in black, faced the grain store with a levelled Schmeisser in his hands. He heard the sound of footsteps some way off and glanced quickly over his shoulder. Four men — the four who had disposed of Spaatz and Hiller — were about thirty yards away: their machine carbines were shoulder slung. The dark figure continued to gaze at the door of the grain store, waited until his ears told him that the approaching group were no more than five yards away, then swung round with his Schmeisser blazing.

Maria said in a subdued tone: 'You play for keeps, don't you? You didn't *have* to kill them.'

'True. True. But, then, I didn't want them to kill me. You don't play footsy with cornered rats. Those are desperate men and you can bet that each one is a trained, efficient and practised killer. I don't much feel like apologising.'

'And no need,' said Ramon who, like his brother, had remained unmoved by the proceedings. 'The only good Nazi is one who has stopped breathing. So. Five guns. What do we do?'

'We stay here because here we're safe. Von Manteuffel may have thirty, forty men, maybe even more. Out in the open we'd be massacred.' He glanced down at the stirring figure of the sentry. 'Ah! Junior is coming to. I think we'll send him for a little walk so that he can apprise his boss that there's been a slight change in the status quo. Remove the rest of his uniform — should give Von Manteuffel quite a turn.'

★ ★ ★

Von Manteuffel was making some notes at his desk when the knock came on the door. He glanced at his watch and smiled in satisfaction. Exactly five minutes had elapsed since his four men had departed, just over two minutes since he had heard the burst of machine-gun fire which could only have signalled the end of the six captives. He called out permission to enter, made a final note, said: 'You are very punctual,' and looked up. His self-satisfied expression surprise vanished and his eyes opened almost impossibly widely. The stumbling figure before him was clad only in his underclothes.

★ ★ ★

The store was deep in shadow. The single lamp had been switched off and what little light there was came from a newly risen moon.

'Fifteen minutes and nothing,' Navarro said. 'Is that good?'

'It's inevitable, I suppose,' Hamilton said. 'We're in darkness. Von Manteuffel's men are exposed, or would be if they showed themselves and they don't dare show themselves. What can they do? Smoke us out if the wind is right? But no wind, so no smoke.'

Ramon said: 'Starve us out?'

'We should live that long.'

* * *

The time crawled by. Apart from Navarro, who stood by the doorway, everyone was lying down. They may or may not have been trying to sleep for some had their eyes shut but were unquestionably wide awake. Navarro said: 'Two hours. That's two hours gone now. Still nothing.'

'Would you mind, watchman? I'm trying to sleep.' Hamilton sat up. 'Don't think I will sleep. They *may* be up to something. I've no cigarettes. Anybody? No?' Serrano proffered a packet. 'I thought you were asleep. Thanks. You know, I wasn't quite sure whether or not to believe what you told me, but I believe you now, if for no other reason than the fact that it has to be as you say. So I guess I owe you an apology.' He paused reflectively: 'Apologising seems to have become a habit with me.'

Ramon said curiously: 'May we know what the present apology is about?'

'Of course. Serrano is government. On the need-to-know principle, I suppose, Colonel Diaz kind of forgot to tell me.'

'Government?'

'Ministry of Culture. Fine Arts.'

'God help us all,' Ramon said. 'I would have thought there were enough genuine vultures in those godforsaken parts without adding culture vultures to the list. What on earth are you doing here, Serrano?'

'That's what I hope to find out.'

'Forthcoming, aren't we? Señor Hamilton?'

'I told you, I only learnt of this a couple of hours ago.'

Ramon looked at him reproachfully. 'Señor Hamilton, you're at it again.'

'At what?'

'Being enigmatic and evasive.'

Hamilton shrugged and said nothing. Serrano said: 'An honest doubt doesn't require an apology.'

'There's a little more to it than that,' Hamilton said. 'I thought you were Hiller's man. Back in Romono, that is, when I first met you. I'm afraid I'm the person who clobbered you. I'll give you back the money I took from your wallet. There's not much I can do about your stiff neck. Forgive me.'

'Forgive, forgive,' Maria said. 'I don't suppose anyone is going to forgive me.'

There was a brief silence, then Hamilton said, mildly enough: 'I have apologised.'

'Apologies and forgiveness are not the same thing and you're clearly of the opinion that my association — that's the nicest way I can put it — was unforgivable. It all depends upon who is doing the judging and casting the first stone. All four of my grandparents

219

died in Auschwitz and the chances are high that it was Von Manteuffel or Spaatz who sent them there. Or both. I suppose the world is tired of hearing about it, but six million Jews did die in the concentration camps. Was I so wrong? I knew if I stayed with Smith long enough he'd lead me to Von Manteuffel and he was the one we really wanted. I knew of only one way of staying with him. So I — we — found Von Manteuffel. Was I so wrong?'

'Tel Aviv?' Hamilton made no attempt to conceal his distaste. 'Another of those barbaric Eichmann show trials?'

'Yes.'

'Von Manteuffel will never leave the Lost City.'

'This Dr Huston,' Serrano said carefully. 'He meant so much? And his daughter?'

'Yes.'

'You were here at the time they — ah — died?'

'Murdered. No. I was in Vienna. But a friend of mine — Jim Clinton — was here. He buried them. He even gave them a tombstone and inscription — burnt on wood with a red-hot poker. Von Manteuffel killed him also — some time later.'

'Vienna?' Maria said. 'Wiesenthal? The Institute?'

Serrano said: 'What's this, young lady?'

'You should watch those slips of the tongue, Mr Serrano, such as calling me a young lady. The Institute is a Jewish central organisation for hunting down war criminals. Based in Austria, not Israel. Mr Hamilton, why can they never let the left hand know what the right is doing?'

'Same old need-to-know principle, I suppose. All that I really know is that I'd a double reason for hunting Von Manteuffel down. I got close to him twice in the Argentine, twice in Chile, once in Bolivia, twice in the Kolonie 555. An elusive character, always on the run, always surrounded by his Nazi thugs. But I've caught up with him.'

'Or the other way around,' Serrano said.

Hamilton remained silent.

'Your friends are buried here?'

'Yes.'

★　★　★

'I'm hungry and I'm thirsty,' Navarro said plaintively. It was half an hour before dawn.

'I am deeply moved by your sufferings,' Hamilton said. 'What's a damned sight more important is that you're alive. I didn't want to depress anyone any more than we already were by saying what was in my mind, but I didn't really think we'd see the night out.'

Ramon said: 'And how could that have been?'

'Quite simple, really. Lots of ways. With a small cannon, a rocket launcher, any kind of anti-aircraft gun or a mortar. They could have directed two or three very nasty rounds of high explosive straight through this open doorway. Maybe the shrapnel would not have got us all, but the concussion in this confined space would have finished us off. Or they could have crawled over the grain store roof from the back and lobbed in a few grenades or a stick or so of blasting powder. The effect would have been the same. Maybe they didn't have any of those materials to hand, which I don't for a moment believe — Von Manteuffel lugs around with him enough weaponry and artillery for an armoured battalion. Maybe the idea just didn't occur to them, which I don't believe either. I think that Von Manteuffel believes, as he has reason to, that we are dangerous in the dark and is waiting for daylight before moving in for the kill.'

Serrano said unhappily: 'It will be daylight quite soon.'

'It will, won't it?' In the first faint glimmering of light Maria, Serrano and Silver

222

stared at Hamilton without comprehension as he extracted the camera from his haversack, opened it, released the flap to display the transceiver, extended an aerial and spoke into the microphone.

'Night-watch,' Hamilton said. 'Night-watch.'

The speaker crackled and the reply was immediate.

'We have you, Night-watch.'

'Now.'

'Now it is. How many vultures?'

'Thirty. Forty. A guess.'

'Repeat after me: Stay under cover. Napalm.'

'Stay under cover. Napalm.' Hamilton switched off. 'Useful, no? Very thoughtful is Colonel Diaz.'

'Napalm!' Ramon said.

'You heard the man.'

'But napalm!'

'Very tough, those airborne commandos. But, no, they don't use it directly. They've no intention of dropping the stuff on us. They ring the area. Not a new technique but very intimidating.'

Hamilton made another switch on the camera and a faint bleeping sound could be heard.

'Homing signal,' Ramon explained to no-one in particular. 'How else do you think they'd ever locate this place?'

'You've got everything organised, haven't you?' Maria sounded slightly bitter. 'Never thought to tell us, did you?'

'Why should I?' Hamilton said indifferently. 'Nobody ever tells me anything.'

'How long will they take to get here?'

'Twenty minutes. No more.'

'And dawn is in about the same time?'

'About.'

'It's starting to get light already. They could still attack before your friends get here.'

'Most unlikely. In the first place, it'll take Von Manteuffel and his minions some time to get organised and if we can't hold them off for a few minutes after that then we've no right to be here in the first place. Secondly, as soon as they hear the sound of the helicopter engines they're going to forget all about us.'

It was becoming quite light now but still the courtyard remained deserted. If Von Manteuffel and his men were preparing to launch an attack they were being extremely discreet about it.

By and by Ramon said: 'Engines. I can hear them now. They're coming in from the south.'

'I don't hear them myself, but if you say they're coming in, then they're coming in. Do you see what I see, Ramon?'

'Yes, indeed. I see a man on the roof of their mess hall with a pair of binoculars to his eyes.

224

He must have good hearing, too. The legs?'

'If you would.'

In his typical one-sweep movement Ramon lifted his rifle and squeezed the trigger. The man with the binoculars collapsed to the roof then, after some seconds, scuttled crab-wise away on two hands and a knee, dragging a useless leg behind him.

Hamilton said: 'Our friend, General Von Manteuffel, must, as they say, be losing his cool or he wouldn't have taken a stupid liberty like that. I don't think we'll be seeing any more sky-watchers.' He paused. 'I can hear them now.'

The sound of the aero engines was now unmistakable and increased rapidly in strength as the craft approached: finally, the rackety clamour of the engines reached an almost intolerable pitch as three large gunships began to descend between the reverberating walls of the cliffsides.

Hamilton said: 'Inside, I think.'

Maria paused in the doorway. 'Okay to look?'

Hamilton pushed her roughly inside and behind a wooden partition where he joined her.

'Napalm, you ninny. Some of that stuff could fly loose.'

'Rockets? Bombs?'

'Jesus! This is an historic monument.'

Moments later, almost having to shout to

make herself heard over the clamour, she said: 'That awful smell.'

'Napalm.'

'Shouldn't we — shouldn't we go out and help them?'

'Help them? We'd only be in their way. Believe me, those lads don't require help of any kind. And has it occurred to you that they'd probably mow us down before we got three paces beyond that doorway? They don't know who we are and airborne commandos have the odd habit of shooting you first and asking who you are afterwards. A little discretion and patience until peace and calm reign again.'

The peace and calm came within two minutes. The sound of the helicopter engines died away. A klaxon sounded, presumably to indicate an all-clear. Not one shot had been fired.

Hamilton said: 'I think the intrepid Captain Hamilton and his gallant crew may now safely risk a peek outside.' They filed out through the open doorway.

Three gunships stood in the courtyard before the ziggurat. The ruins of the ancient city were ringed with smoke from the still burning napalm. At least fifty commandos, looking very tough and very competent and certainly armed to the teeth, had their guns trained on about three dozen of Von Manteuffel's followers, while four commandos, one of them carrying a carton of handcuffs which had been brought along for the purpose, moved along them securing their wrists behind their backs. In the forefront of the captives was Von Manteuffel himself, already handcuffed.

As Hamilton and the others reached the centre of the courtyard an army officer advanced to meet them.

'Mr Hamilton?' he said. 'Major Ramirez. At your service.'

'You have already been of more than enough service.' They shook hands. 'We are most grateful. That really was efficient.'

'My men are disappointed,' Ramirez said. 'We had expected a rather more — ah — challenging training exercise. You wish to leave now?'

'An hour, if we may.' Hamilton pointed to Von Manteuffel. 'I'd like to speak to that man.'

Von Manteuffel was brought forward between two soldiers. His face was grey and without expression.

Hamilton said: 'Major, this is Major-General Wolfgang Von Manteuffel of the S.S.'

'The last of the infamous Nazi war-time criminals, no? I do not have to shake hands?'

'No.' Hamilton looked consideringly at Von Manteuffel. 'You have, of course, murdered Colonel Spaatz. And Hiller. Along, of course, with Dr Huston his daughter, scores of Muscias and God knows how many others. To every road there is an end. With your permission, Major, there are a couple of things I would like to show Von Manteuffel.'

Accompanied by a group of soldiers armed with shovels, powerful electric torches and two large battery-powered floodlamps, they made their way towards the base of the ziggurat.

'This ziggurat is unique,' Hamilton said. 'Every other known one is solid throughout. This one has been hollowed out and honeycombed like the great Egyptian ones. Please follow me.'

He led them along a winding, crumbling passage-way until they came to a low, vaulted cavern, smooth-walled, with no further passageway leading from it. The floor was deeply covered with broken fragments of rock and a great deal of gravel to a depth of between one and two feet. Hamilton spoke to Ramirez and indicated a particular area: eight soldiers with shovels immediately began to excavate this area. In a short time an area of about six feet by six had been cleared to reveal a square slab of stone with an inset iron ring at either end. Crowbars were inserted into the rings and the slab, not without some considerable difficulty, lifted clear.

A shallow flight of stairs led down from the opening in the cavern floor. They moved down these, along a rough-hewn passage and halted before a heavy wooden door.

Hamilton said: 'Well, Serrano, this is where you come into your own. As for you, Von Manteuffel, let your last reflections on earth be the most ironic you've ever had. You'd have given your heart and your soul — if you ever had one — for what lies beyond that door but you sat atop it all those years and never dreamed it was there.'

He paused, as if deep in thought, then said: 'It's a mite dark in there. There are no windows or lights. If you would be so kind, Major, as to have your men switch on all torches and floodlamps. I'm afraid the air will also be a bit musty, but it won't kill you. Ramon, Navarro, give me a hand with this door.'

The door proved to be reluctant to yield, but with a sepulchral creaking sound, yield it eventually did. Hamilton took one of the floodlights and passed through, the others crowding close behind.

The large square cavern was hewn from the

solid rock. All four sides had stepped rock shelves cut into them to a depth of fifteen inches. The spectacle was astonishing, far beyond any belief: the entire cavern gleamed and glittered with thousands upon thousands of artifacts in solid gold.

There were bowls, chalices, plates, all in solid gold. There were helmets, shields, plaques, necklets, busts and figurines, all in solid gold. There were bells, flutes, ocarinas, rope-chains, vases, breastplates, openwork headdresses, filigree masks and knives, all in solid gold. There were monkeys, alligators, snakes, eagles and condors, pelicans and vultures and innumerable jaguars, all in solid gold. And for good measure there were half a dozen open boxes, sparkling and glittering with an untold fortune in precious stones, more than half of them emeralds. It was a treasure house inconceivably far beyond the dreams of avarice.

It seemed as if the awed silence would last for ever. Serrano, at last, was the first to speak.

'The lost treasure of the Indies. The El Dorado of a million dreams. The Spanish always believed that some vanished tribe had taken with them a huge treasure trove such as this: mankind has believed in the myth ever since and thousands have lost their lives in the search for El Dorado. But it was no myth, no myth.'

Serrano, it was clear, was scarcely capable of believing the evidence of his eyes.

'It was a myth, all right,' Hamilton said. 'But the golden treasure was there all right but everybody looked for it in the wrong place — up in the Guianas. And they all looked for the wrong thing — they thought it was royal Inca gold. But it wasn't. The people who made these were the Quimbaya of the Cauca valley, the greatest masters of the goldsmith's art in history. For them gold had no commercial value, it was solely a thing of beauty.'

'And the Spaniards would have melted the lot and sent it back to Spain in ingot form. Mr Hamilton, you have done the world of art an immeasurable service. And you were the only non-Indian alive who knew of this. You could have been the richest man alive.'

Hamilton shrugged. 'Once a Quimbaya, always a Quimbaya.'

Ramirez said: 'What will become of this?'

'It is to be a national museum. The rightful owners, the Muscias, will return and become the custodians. Few people, I'm afraid, will ever see this — just accredited scholars from all over the world and but a few of those at a time. The Brazilian

231

government — who don't even know the location of this place yet — is determined that the Muscias, what's left of them, will not be destroyed by civilisation.'

Hamilton looked at Von Manteuffel who was gazing, trance-like, at the immense fortune that had lain beneath his feet. He was stunned. But then so, too, was everyone else.

Hamilton said: 'Von Manteuffel.' Von Manteuffel turned his head slowly and looked at him like a sightless man.

'Come. I have one last thing to show you.'

Hamilton led the way into another, much smaller cavern. Side by side at the far end lay two stone sarcophagi. Above each was a plain pine board with poker-burnt inscriptions.

Hamilton said: 'A friend of mine did those, Von Manteuffel. Jim Clinton. Remember Jim Clinton? You should. After all, you murdered him shortly afterwards. Read them. Read them aloud.'

Still in the same odd sightless fashion Von Manteuffel looked slowly around, looked at Hamilton, and read: 'Dr Hannibal Huston. R.I.P.'

'And the other?' Hamilton said.

'Lucy Huston Hamilton. Beloved wife of John Hamilton. R.I.P.'

Everyone stared at Hamilton. Shocked comprehension came slowly but it came.

Von Manteuffel said: 'I am a dead man.'

Hamilton, with Ramon and Navarro, Von Manteuffel and the others trudging along closely behind, made their way to a helicopter which was parked at the edge of the courtyard only yards from the rim of the plateau. Suddenly Von Manteuffel, wrists still handcuffed behind his back, ran towards the edge of the cliff. Ramon started after him, but Hamilton caught him by the arm.

'Let him be. You heard what he said. He's a dead man.'

We do hope that you have enjoyed reading this large print book.

Did you know that all of our titles are available for purchase?

We publish a wide range of high quality large print books including:
Romances, Mysteries, Classics
General Fiction
Non Fiction and Westerns

Special interest titles available in large print are:
The Little Oxford Dictionary
Music Book
Song Book
Hymn Book
Service Book

Also available from us courtesy of Oxford University Press:
Young Readers' Dictionary
(large print edition)
Young Readers' Thesaurus
(large print edition)

For further information or a free brochure, please contact us at:
Ulverscroft Large Print Books Ltd.,
The Green, Bradgate Road, Anstey,
Leicester, LE7 7FU, England.
Tel: (00 44) 0116 236 4325
Fax: (00 44) 0116 234 0205